Dust Between the Stitches

We owe a lot to the Greatest Generation!

Cleo Lampos

By Cleo Lampos

Layout and Cover Design by Penoaks Publishing, http://penoaks.com

Dedicated to my parents
Ina and Jesse
Who lived in the Dust Bowl during the 1930's
And to my sister
Maralyn Louise
Who encouraged the writing of this novel from the beginning

Appreciation to the artists involved in this novel
Maralyn Dettmann and Kaeley Clark

SEPTEMBER, 1938

Chapter 1

"I won't let this happen."

Addy Meyers crumpled the bank document in her fist and pressed her lips tightly together. "Grandpa will not suffer this loss. Not while I can still inhale one more breath of mountain air." Tension pearled down her spine, straightening her. "This is just too much. That banker needs to be told how to treat people with respect."

She spun on her heel and marched out of the kitchen, clutching the paper ball in her right hand. With her left fist, she shoved the screen door open. It slammed and bounced back at her.

"Ouch!" A deep voice bellowed.

Staring through the screen mesh, Addy gazed at a man dressed in denim who covered his nose. Dust clung to his shirt and jeans. The visor of the cloth hat on his head held a layer of powder like all of the

Colorado landscape in this unrelenting dry spell of 1938. His clothes were too new for him to be a hobo.

Where did he come from?

"Did you ever think to stand clear of a door?" Addy slid onto the porch while letting the screen door close after her. She peered upward to see the man's dark brown eyes.

"Never thought one would whack me in the face before." The man back-stepped. "Your grandpa doesn't move so fast that I ever needed to worry about being hit by a door."

"What do you know about my grandpa? And how do you know that I am his granddaughter?"

Addy's suspicious eyes peered past the man, searching shadows in the dusty farm yard, but found no one else among the chickens who scratched at the dirt to unearth a morsel. The windmill creaked in the hot breeze. There were no signs of anything unusual. Except for this man planted firmly on the top step of the stoop. A man who knew her grandpa, but she didn't recall her grandpa talking about him.

"Good morning. The name is Jess. Jess Dettmann." He snatched the hat off his head, spilling chestnut brown hair over the tops of his ears. His smile was a switch that sparked twinkles in his eyes. "Well, now, there are two questions you're asking. I can answer those. You are Addy Meyers, and you came here last week to be with your Grandpa George since his wife died recently. Help him with those young'uns they adopted, RiverLyn and Billy."

"How do you know so much about my family?" Addy slatted her eyes. Why should she trust this fellow? Was he a scam artist like the thieves who plagued the poor back in Topeka? A n'er do well like those who preyed on her mother?

"When I'm in the Greeley area, I rent the old log cabin in back of the bushes along the creek. Put my gear in there last night when I talked to Grandpa George. He was out for a stroll in the moonlight, or so he said. Your grandma, Martha, boarded me with the tastiest cornbread this side of the Rockies. I just got back from a job on the Big Thompson

River. Will be digging irrigation ditches for the beet farmers getting ready for next spring's planting as soon as the harvest is gathered."

"Well, don't expect me to do any cooking for you, Mr. Dettmann. Just because my grandma did, that doesn't mean that I'm willing to be chief cook and bottle washer. I will be—"

"Teaching over in the Running Creek School. Yeah, Grandpa George keeps me up to date. And my name is Jess. Just call me Jess."

"Well, Mr. Jess." Addy tried to avoid looking into his brown eyes as she spoke. He was the sort of guy who could melt an ice block in January. When she came to Colorado's foothills, she didn't expect to meet a good-looking fellow. But the handsome ones usually meant trouble. They wormed their way into her mother's life, then took her money and disappeared. "Don't mean to dash on, but I need to talk to Grandpa."

"That's okay, Addy. Don't worry about making any meal today. I'm taking RiverLyn and Billy fishing for some walleyes for our supper. Least I can do." Jess smiled before walking over to three bamboo fishing poles leaning against the chicken's fence. He picked them up, slung them over his shoulder, straightened his hat, and sauntered off toward the creek. Addy's face heated as she recognized the song he whistled. "You Must Have Been a Beautiful Baby."

Addy spotted the children throwing a baseball near the water's edge. *Smack*. RiverLyn leaned into the catch, then immediately fired it back to Billy. *Smack*. Into his hand and out again so fast the ball was a blur. After playing with them once, Addy went away with tingling fingers and red hands. For skinny kids, they had sinewy arm muscles. They played baseball better than the kids in Topeka any day.

She continued to watch as Jess rounded the chicken coop toward the lanky ten-year-old boy and his serious eight-year-old sister. By their joyful whoops and hollers, it was apparent that they knew Jess. Addy did not stop watching the trio until they disappeared in the bushes along the creek.

Wish life was as easy for me as it is for all of them. Pity enveloped Addy the way dust clouds deepened and consumed entire Oklahoma cities in their gravelly fury. Since she arrived several days ago, things had not gone as well as she expected. The children remembered little of her from years ago when she and her mother came from Kansas to visit. Addy's mother refused to accept these orphaned children as siblings, so their stay had been strained, to say the least. Guess that made RiverLyn her aunt, and Billy, her uncle. The thought curved Addy's lips into a grin.

Even though she passed the two year teaching program with high marks, she didn't feel prepared to teach in a one-room schoolhouse, much less fill shoes as big as Grandma's. Billy and RiverLyn resented Addy taking Grandma's place after her death. But who could blame them? She wasn't ready to be a teacher or a substitute mother.

She glanced down at the crumpled paper in her hand and pressed it crinkly smooth against the gray, wind-blown boards of the porch railing. Squinting her eyes against the blazing sun, she slid her moccasins through the fine dirt, raising tiny dust clouds around her ankles. She followed the scraggly path leading to the garden where she spotted Grandpa hoeing weeds between the rows of green beans. A wiry, thin gent with a shock of gray hair under his straw hat, Grandpa still maintained muscle mass in his biceps. His grip on the hoe remained firm, and his attack on the weeds was sure.

Passing a scarecrow created from frayed garments, Addy chuckled to herself. A remnant from Kansas. Grandma always had a scarecrow, even here in Colorado. At the thought of her grandma, a pain stabbed her middle, just like the way it did on the day she heard of grandma's swift heart attack and death. One more loss in a long chain of losses linked together. But she'd stop this one. She shook the paper as she gripped it tighter in her fist.

"Hey, there, Addy. I spotted you comin'. Mighty warm for September, ain't it?" Grandpa straightened. "What's that in your hand?"

"I think you have an idea. It's from the bank in town." She breathed in the air laced with fine rock residue, air that dehydrated one's body and withered one's soul.

He reached for the letter. "Probably addressed to me. Yep. Says George right here in the heading, not Addy. You takin' over my mail now?" Smiling, he leaned on his hoe, but the tone in his voice conveyed a serious edge.

"Okay, chew me out for opening it. That letter says you have to come up with the back taxes or the bank will foreclose on you. Two thousand dollars. That's a lot of money." Addy waved the paper in front of his eyes. "Look."

"I know what it says. They's been sending those to a bunch of us farmers and ranchers around here. Don't mean too much. They can't take all of our homesteads, now can they?"

Addy winced. "You know they can. They took my mother's house and nearly the whole block we lived on back in Topeka. Yes, the bank will buy up every bit of the land you worked on all these years. It's 1938, and the banks have just about foreclosed on the whole United States."

"Why, I've known the bank president since Martha and me settled here ten years ago. He's my friend." Grandpa pulled off his straw hat and wiped his brow with a handkerchief.

"Doesn't matter a bit, Grandpa. Banks have no hearts. But I won't let them take this land from you. I'll find a way. Wait and see." She pointed to a number at the bottom of the paper. "Two thousand dollars in arrears. How could you get so far behind?" She paused to draw in her breath. "No more losses. I can't lose one more thing. Not this farm." Gritting her teeth in irritation, she seethed. She'd only been here for a week, and now all this difficulty to face. Plus, a new job.

'Just one dust storm after another. Dried up every crop I put in. Thinned out the herd so we hardly have enough cattle to sell to keep current. Jess Dettmann got me plantin' sugar beets for a cash crop. He dug the irrigation ditches with his dragline as his room and board." Grandpa cupped his hand over his eyes and gazed at acres of straight rows of beets that stretched out across the sandy soil. "We'll see how much the crop is worth this fall." He plopped the straw hat back over his thick, gray hair.

"Yes. I just met this Jess person. Funny, you never talked about him. Gold digger, if you ask me."

Grandpa paused, staring at her. "Didn't ask you." With that, he picked up his hoe and sliced the stem off a prickly weed.

Addy pressed her lips together so she wouldn't say something she regretted. Shuffling back to the weathered house, she decided to water the raised bed garden. She pumped water into a galvanized watering can. Grandpa's homestead was unusual for the area in the fact that he had a well in addition to a creek running on his property. In this decade of drought, it made all the difference between making it or losing everything. Every drop of liquid meant life. Addy carried the precious water to the thirsty plants until her arms ached and the agitation drained from her body.

Grandpa was washing up in the sink when she stepped into the kitchen.

"Thought I would rustle up some vittles." Addy tied back her shoulder-length hair in a blue ribbon that matched her eyes.

"Your grandma would have said that." Grandpa's voice wavered.

"Grandma had a saying for so many things. Now, how about you get me the ingredients for biscuits, and I'll get the oven heated up." Addy placed sticks in the wood-burning stove, then struck a match.

She circled her waist with her grandma's apron. Before long, she had biscuits baking in the oven and flour splattered on the kitchen table. The scent of the dough browning filled the air. Her mouth salivated as the smell lingered in her nostrils. Grandma always graced the evening meal with biscuits. A real comfort food.

"What do you want from the pantry, Addy? We still have the pickled beets, peaches, applesauce, and pickles that Grandma put up."

"Pickled beets. That will go well with the tomatoes and cucumbers you picked from the garden this morning." Addy sliced the testaments to Grandpa's green thumb. "Remember when I came here as a little girl, and I helped Grandma can jellies from the strawberries, blueberries, and currants in the garden?"

"Those were summers we looked forward to because we loved gettin' you out of Topeka. I loved my daughter, but the way she acted and raised you caused your Grandma and I to pray a lot."

Addy's mind switched to her party-loving mother who brought home men who smelled of beer. She changed the subject. "One summer I went to church with you, and we sang 'I'll Fly Away' and clapped our hands till they burned. And don't think I didn't notice your eyes tear up whenever the choir sang 'Will the Circle Be Unbroken?'. Those songs always have extra meaning to me." *God, I need the comfort of music in my life right now.*

"We had RiverLyn and Billy at that time. They wiggled on the pew, but you helped us keep them under control. Your grandma and I were blessed. We stood on the train platform in Kansas and greeted the last orphan train to come through in 1930. Gettin' these two street urchins from New York City gave us a new lease on life. Brought some excitement into this quiet house."

"I loved coming here and helping out each summer." More than anyone would ever guess.

The sound of children's laughter in the distance drew Addy from her thoughts.

RiverLyn burst through the screen door, thick brown braids bouncing on her shoulders, her sundress hanging loosely on her thin body. "Look, Addy! We caught them with Jess! We're eatin' fish tonight!"

Billy followed his sister. He held an oilcloth in his outstretched hands with three medium fish filleted and ready to fry.

Billy inhaled loud gasps of air. "Mm. Biscuits. You make 'em just like Grandma used to." The lad licked his chops.

"That's about five things that you can make now, Addy." RiverLyn shook her head. "Guess we won't starve if ya keep learnin' to cook more than oatmeal and eggs."

"I've never cooked fish." Addy smiled at the youngster with the gangly limbs. "Maybe Grandpa can fry these up."

"I mentioned I would make supper tonight. If you don't mind, ma'am, I do believe my fried fish is as good as that being served in the finest hotels in Denver." Jess filled the frame of the door, his hat in his hand, a shock of thick brown hair falling from a side part. "RiverLyn,

Billy, and I enjoy cooking together." He nodded toward Addy. "If you don't mind."

She stared at him, sizing up his intentions. So far, the few nigglings in her brain had not panned into anything sinister. She shrugged. "I look forward to tonight's main dish."

Before taking off her apron, she pulled the golden brown biscuits from the oven and set them on the windowsill to cool. She strolled into the hall and to the bedroom she shared with RiverLyn. Excited voices blended in the kitchen with the metallic scrape of the iron frying pan on the wood-burning cook stove. Addy closed the bedroom door.

Not much to do until supper. Addy knew RiverLyn would set the table. As an eight-year-old, RiverLyn liked the responsibility of getting food on the table. She had been a great help to Grandma, especially in the last year when the older woman slowed down a bit.

Addy surveyed the room. On the bed lay the quilt with the pattern of wedding rings stitched on it. The one that Grandma made for her hope chest before marrying Grandpa. Addy slept under that quilt as a child when she lived with her grandparents while her mother took off for long vacations without her.

She brushed the wooden-slatted headboard Grandpa constructed from a cherry tree that blew down. Addy took a deep breath. How she missed her grandma: her patience, her wisdom, her love. Unlike Grandpa, she was never curt. Addy glanced around the tiny bedroom. She needed something to do so her thoughts would settle.

Maybe a good time to mend the knees of Billy's overalls. That boy tore through clothes like a greased pig at the fair. Grandmother's sewing basket sat in the corner near a straight-back chair. Taking off the basket's lid, she picked up the material lying on the top. Grandma folded the muslin in precise squares. Unfolding it, she gasped at the appliquéd design.

Sunbonnet Sue. The newest quilting pattern, button stitched with an exactness that only Grandma brought to sewing projects. But, the heart-stopping aspect of the quilt square, which she surmised by the twelve-inch measurement, lay in the material for Sunbonnet Sue's dress and bonnet. The red-striped cotton came from the last dress Grandma made for Addy before she graduated from high school. Grandma formed the quilt piece's solid bonnet from the red cloth that she used to make piping for the dress. Addy traced the appliqué as a tear splashed over her cheek. Grandma always took the scraps of life and made beauty out of them.

Losses. More losses. Seemed like extra ones rising regular like the blazing sun on the horizon. Addy slumped. She gazed on a plaque hanging over the dresser. *Only one life and soon 'tis past. Only what's done for Christ will last.* Her grandparents believed that motto and lived it. That is the legacy that Addy longed to follow rather than her mother's wandering ways.

"Comin' to eat, Addy?" RiverLyn's sweet voice brought Addy back to the task at hand.

Refolding the quilt square, she placed it inside the sewing basket. She answered as she squared her shoulders. "Be right there."

So much to do to meet the tax payment. So much at stake. Responsibility pressed as heavy as mountain boulders.

Chapter 2

The sun broke bright and clear over the sugar beet fields on Sunday morning.

The Lord's Day. Jess always thought of Sunday as the Lord's Day, because he'd gone to church on that day since birth. Up until about a year ago, on Sunday, he would have attired himself in a wool-blended suit custom made for him from a choice of navy blue, gray, or black. A hand-painted silk tie selected for the season from an array of ties adorned a white cotton shirt starched and ironed by the laundress down the street. The shoes gleamed from the buffing by the bootblack, an enterprising young boy who stood on the corner hoping to make a few pennies. His appearance met the expectations of those he tried to impress.

But the man who needed that kind of approval no longer existed. Glancing in the mirror at the suntanned man who shaved his own face now, Jess smiled with satisfaction. He'd made a total break with the past.

Addy would never know that person who traveled here to stay with George and Martha. The man who required hard work to keep his mind focused and free from bitterness.

So, today he pulled on dark gray dress slacks and buttoned a white shirt without a tie. He slipped on ankle boots made of cow's leather. Wetting his hands, he slicked his hair back from the side part. Grabbing his Bible, he jumped into his '33 Ford pickup and headed down the road, leaving a cloud of dirt behind him. Soon the foothills of the mountains drew closer. On the side of the road, scraggly trees stood upright by clutching dry soil. Tumble weeds pressed against boulders.

Turning off the gravel road, Jess drove over ruts until he spotted smoke trains winding skyward above the trees. He followed the wheel tracks until the first tent appeared. Hooverville, that's what the residents called this amassing of tents and makeshift structures. He reckoned Addy would have some reservations about his spending time with down-and-outers like these in Hooverville. But this is where Jesus wanted him on a Sunday morning. Jess pulled his pickup off the dirt road.

"Hey, it's the preacher." A tall, gaunt man sat on a three-legged wooden stool in front of a shack made of cardboard, odd pieces of wood, and tar paper. "Must be time for the service." The man walked over to the Ford as Jess cut the engine.

"Howdy, Calvin. Got your voice all tuned up? Need you to lead the singing again." He lost more weight. Things must be getting worse. Didn't know how they could. Calvin took on a gray pallor.

"Got the band ready. Woody on guitar, Grace on the violin, and Ted said he'd come in on his harmonica when it fit. We practiced some new numbers, and Ted makes a nice transition between verses with his harmonica. Wait till you hear it, Preacher."

"Call me Jess. I look forward to the music and singing in this town named for the President of the United States." Jess winked at Calvin. "How have things been going?"

Calvin's voice deepened. "One more family left for California. They packed up everything and piled into their Model T. We all gave a nickel so they would have gas to get there."

"Are they hoping to find jobs in the fruit groves?"

"We warned them about those signs on the California border telling anyone without a job to stay out. But they jist don't listen. Desperation does strange things to a man's common sense. I fear for that family. They got two young'uns." Calvin shook his head.

Jess's chest tightened. Over the years, he witnessed what desperation drove men to do. And women. And even children. An accumulation of that kind of despair led to him leaving, well, leaving a battle he no longer wanted to fight. Heaviness dragged on his feet.

By the time Jess and Calvin strolled to the eastern edge of the hundred or more shanties that comprised Hooverville, a group of people followed them like the children in the story of the Pied Piper. At the flattened area of sand, other residents balanced long planks on flat-top rocks to make benches.

Jess slapped the back of a thin man known for his whittling of wooden statues. "How are the wood chips flying, Al?"

"Great, Preacher. I sold a dog statue and an eagle in town the other day."

"That's good news, Al. Hope you find a market for your work. It's exceptional."

Al's cheeks blazed as his mouth curved upward.

A young woman clasped Jess's hand. "Thank you for the words at our baby's funeral. It's been a while, but the scripture you read still comforts me." Her eyes moistened as she slipped into the gathering crowd.

Jess gulped back his own tears. Over the years, he'd seen too many children buried, and it left him somber. Nothing changed in this poverty-stricken place. He continued greeting and shaking the hands of those nearby.

Calvin welcomed people until he and Jess worked their way to the front. The women and children already occupied the first row seating.

Woody, Grace, and Ted carried their instruments to the front, and started playing a lively rendition of "I'll Fly Away". Clapping and some foot stomping added rhythm to the song. Calvin joined the musicians while Jess moved to the side. After several minutes, the song ended in jubilation, and the musicians transitioned into another favorite.

How did they do this? These people owned nothing. Nothing. Yet, here they were, singing with more passion than the well-to-do-congregation he shepherded back in the city.

Does it take hard times to move people from their apathy to a closer walk with you, Lord? Help me as I preach your words that will heal their souls. Give them strength for the hardships that they have endured and fresh ones coming up.

Finally, the last musical chord faded into the sounds of birds chirping in their nests. Jess opened his Bible as he stood in front of the people seated on plank benches. A hush fell over the group. The swish of wind on dirt reminded him of the dry conditions around him. An eagle circled overhead. A hint of pine oil from a stand of evergreens wafted in their direction.

"Hear the Word of the Lord." Jess paused and gained eye contact with the congregation. "Today, my message is found in Luke 10, verses 25 to 37. Grace, will you read this passage to us?"

Taking Jess's Bible, Grace read with expression.

"Thank you, Grace. Now, this is a familiar story about the Good Samaritan. At one time, each of us played that role of the helper, the Good Samaritan. The one who took care of the needy. But times have changed with the economic depression we are in. Folks have lost jobs and homes. They are the down-and-out. It is an uncomfortable role and easy to chafe at it."

Jess preached from his heart, asking the men to do everything they could for themselves, but to realize they still needed help, needed neighbors, and needed God. He prayed, "Heavenly Father, I don't want to face my weaknesses. But I am a helpless man who must depend on You and others. Thank you, God, for every time someone supports me. This morning we plead for the couple and their two children who left for what they hope is the Promised Land. Give them daily food. Protect them. Send a Good Samaritan on their path. Let them feel your compassionate arms around them in their need. Amen."

The people sat in silence with bowed heads as Jess asked, "Calvin, will you lead us one more time in that new song? The words feed my soul. Can I hear an amen to that?"

With a loud "amen" in his ears, Jess stepped to the back of the audience, and viewed the residents of Hooverville one more time as they harmonized "Just a Closer Walk with Thee."

Jake and his wife and two little ones. They just buried the baby in a tiny pine box. They looked like skeletons themselves.

Roy and his wife, past the age of work, clinging to life.

Hal and his son, so sad since his wife went crazy and they put her in an asylum.

How could a person lose everything and still believe? All of these people were regulars in the Wednesday soup kitchen at the Catholic church. No jobs. No hope. *Lord, give them a walk with you. You alone can life their burdens. Let it be. Dear Lord, let it be.*

Jess left Hooverville with a heavy heart, just like he did every Sunday. What kind of future did these people have in the foothills with winter coming? What did God expect him to do with so much injustice perpetrated on the poor and orphaned? He tried once to make things right in the world, and looked where that got him.

Chapter 3

Jess paced the wooden floor of the log cabin until his nerves drove him out the screen door into the starry night. The moon hung over the mountains, a silver ball reflecting light into the darkness. Countless stars pierced through the black with stellar brightness. The night sky always soothed his soul. As Jess gazed at God's creation, his breathing leveled out. The tension in his muscles relaxed. The years of stress took their toll, but life in this log cabin reversed some of the effects. He didn't look too bad for a man in his late twenties.

Jess loved coming to George and Martha's homestead. He missed Martha. She always viewed life from the sunny side and kept him more optimistic than his nature allowed. And then there was the surprise of Addy Meyers being here. She brought something new to the family he had grown so fond of. Martha spoke of the granddaughter she helped to raise off and on through the years. But he expected Addy to be perhaps a teenager, not a grown woman with a detached disposition. Maybe she just needed to settle in.

Reluctantly, Jess returned to the log cabin's main room and lit a kerosene lamp. Laying out large sheets of paper, he drew in the irrigation system for the Hulford's ranch down the road apiece. Line by line, he measured the spaces needed, the connections to the source, the maximization of the acreage. With each pencil stroke, Jess pulled himself back into the work that he loved, that gave his life meaning.

In a world with so much loss of land, dignity, and worth, his micrometer eyes dug straight irrigation ditches that provided marginal ranchers with a cash crop: sugar beets. Who would have predicted that his love of geometry could be so useful? Yawning, he laid down his compass and protractor, rubbing his sleepy eyes with rough fingertips, but worried thoughts of Grandpa George furrowed his brow. Would the irrigation ditches help bring in a harvest sufficient to pay the bank? Would Grandpa George be one more victim of the bank's foreclosure? What else could be done?

# # #

The rooster heralded dawn with a screeching clamor. Jess caught the first rays slicing across the mature beet fields as he did when Martha was alive. He headed over to George's house, let himself in, and stoked a fire in the cook stove. He chuckled as he recalled how Martha taught him to start the coffee and slice the bread before stirring up a skillet of scrambled eggs.

He heard light footsteps behind him.

"Billy." Jess grinned as he glanced over his shoulder at the boy in patched overalls. "Make the toast. I sliced some bread for it." Jess dished out the cooked eggs onto a platter, setting them on the table.

Billy stared at Jess. "I've never made toast. Ain't that woman's work? Shouldn't Addy do that?"

"Well, your grandma rustled up great cinnamon toast, but I think you can do it too." Jess handed Billy a bowl with butter in it. "Now, add some sugar, a few teaspoons of cinnamon, and a dash of vanilla."

Reaching to the shelf with spices, Billy gathered all he needed. "What next?"

"Stir it up, and slick it on this bread. Thick, slick it thick. Then put it on the cookie sheet and into the oven."

Soon the aroma of caramelized cinnamon hung in the kitchen air. Jess pulled the tin sheet full of toast from the oven and piled the toast on a plate.

Grandpa George shuffled into the kitchen. "Mornin' to you all." He poured himself a cup of coffee from the pot on the cook stove. "Smells great, Jess. Sounds like the girls are just about to sail in. Quick, sit down, Billy. You, too, Jess."

The men seated themselves as RiverLyn walked from the hall into the kitchen. Her hair was freshly braided. She wore a clean, pink dress with lace on the collar, one of Grandma's creations from sugar sacks. Addy followed. Jess noticed the grace of her neck and shoulders when her hair was pulled back in a thick bun. The blue-flowered dress floated on her thin body. He sat and grinned.

Her cheeks reddened. "You made breakfast. Isn't that my job?"

"You girls were sleepin' in, and on the first day of school too." Grandpa teased. "Here, join us. Jess scrambled up some eggs to go with Billy's toast. God is good."

Jess noticed the smile on Addy's lips turned to a tight press when Grandpa George talked about God's goodness. He almost didn't hear Grandpa George ask him to say grace.

"Yes, I will." Jess bowed his head, pausing to gather his thoughts as the womenfolk settled in their chairs. Finally, he sensed the stillness around the table while the chickens clucked in the yard. *Yes, God is good.* "Dear Lord, thank you for the abundance of food you have given to us in these desperate times. Bless Miss Meyers as she begins her teaching at the school. Help RiverLyn and Billy to be good students. Amen."

"You forgot me, Jess. Guess I don't need no blessing. My life has been blessed enough all these years. Pass the toast, Billy." Grandpa George reached out for the plate.

Jess winced at the remark. How could he have forgotten Grandpa George?

"Are you nervous, Addy?" RiverLyn stuffed a forkful of eggs into her mouth.

"Yes, I suppose I am. Went over yesterday to make sure everything was in order, so guess that will have to do. Not much in the school for supplies. Found a cabinet with slates and chalk. Some notebooks left over from last year, I suspect. Thank goodness for the McGuffey Readers and the new reading series for the first graders."

"Never was much supplies." Billy spoke with his cheeks full, then gulped. "Watch out for them eighth grade boys. They can be mean." He used his forearm as a napkin.

"I'm sure I will be able to take care of myself." Addy patted her slicked-back hair.

Jess caught the frown that RiverLyn shot at Billy.

"Do you always make breakfast for the family when you are staying in the log cabin?" Addy dabbed the corners of her mouth with her napkin.

"No, just today. I was up and thought it would help everyone get off to a good start. Most of the time, I have to get to the fields at the crack of dawn to start my work. You probably won't even see much of me, because I have a heavy schedule before harvest." Jess detected a sigh, maybe one of relief, from Addy.

"Need to pack a lunch in the lard buckets." She rose from her chair and headed for the bread box. "How about jelly sandwiches from Grandma's strawberry preserves?"

Jess watched as Billy and RiverLyn wrapped their lunches in cloth napkins and sealed them in the metal pails. Martha trained them well. He picked up the dishes.

"Don't you worry about doin' dishes." Grandpa George spoke as he pulled out the wash pan. "My pleasure to do the clean-up. Now, all of you, skedaddle." He motioned to the door.

Billy and RiverLyn barreled through the door, letting the screen door slam. Addy sighed as she stepped onto the porch. Jess followed closely, then matched her steps down the lane.

"I'm going to pray for you today, Addy. That you'll get off to a good start with this class."

Addy stopped walking. Her back stiffened. "I'll be okay." Then, she hurried to catch up with RiverLyn and Billy.

Why does she brace every time I mention the Lord? What is keeping her from God? Jess watched the trio until they disappeared among the dirt piles.

# # #

Addy tried to ignore the snickers from the three tallest boys in the classroom. Seated together in the back row, arms crossed, defiance written all over their faces. Judging from the boys' postures and the nervous smiles on the younger students, this class held challenges she never faced as a student teacher in Topeka. An uncomfortable swirl of bile from her stomach lodged in her throat. She swallowed.

Eighteen students. Most rode horses to the one-room school house and tethered the animals under the trees. A few children got rides on buckboards. The big boys walked together in a tight bunch. No one came by car.

The boys wore overalls. The girls wore dresses made from feed-sack material. Many slid oversized shoes on the floor, footwear borrowed from a sibling for the first day of school. All carried lard buckets and one pencils, but no other supplies.

This is so different from my teacher training class in Topeka. I'm going to miss that small library and the children who brought pencils, scissors, paper, and a paint set. These children have nothing. Thank goodness for the large box of chalk in the teacher's desk and boards on every wall of the room.

Addy gulped before speaking, borrowing time to focus her mind. "Welcome to Running Creek School. My name is Miss Meyers, and I am going to be your new teacher this year."

"We had two last year," the red-headed eighth grader informed her from the last row.

The lanky lad next to Red leaned back on the bench. "They was all young like you. Didn't last long." All three boys chuckled. The younger children squirmed. RiverLyn and Billy stared at the floor.

"Well, we will see how long any of us last. But, for now, I have a book that I am going to read to you. I bought it before coming here to teach. The title is *And to Think That I Saw It on Mulberry Street.* The author is Dr. Seuss, and this is the only book he has written."

For the next ten minutes, a hush fell on the classroom as the students leaned forward to hear every word she read. Even the eighth grade boys sat without making a sound as her voice flowed with the rhythm and rhyme of the story. When she finished, the class groaned in unison, disappointed the book had ended.

A warm flush reddened her cheeks as she basked in the approval.

"Read some more." A thin girl with stringy, sun-bleached hair begged. She put her hand to her mouth and coughed from deep somewhere inside of her. Addy read the name tag on her desk. Katrina.

"Tomorrow." Addy set the book on the chalkboard railing "Now, everyone, look at the board. Find the math problems for your grade level and copy them on the slates I put on your shelves. When you have computed the answers, raise your hands. RiverLyn, would you come and help our youngest children write their numbers and count?" Addy promised to tutor RiverLyn each evening to keep up her skills if she helped out with the teaching during class time.

Addy stepped around the room, glancing over the shoulders of the students as they copied the problems, then added, subtracted, multiplied, or divided. RiverLyn counted fingers with two first graders. The eighth graders sat with their arms folded.

"You need to get your slates out and try some of those equations." Addy nodded toward the blackboard. "Just review today. We want to get our brains turning after a long summer."

"Our brains are just fine. Don't need no review." The surly redhead was the ringleader.

"Won't do us no good to learn all this stuff anyways." The lanky sidekick predictably rolled his eyes.

"How is that so?"

Red answered. "Can't get a job needin' learnin'. Where you been? Eighth grade ed-je-cation is good enough to work a ranch or maybe lay ties for the railroad."

"Math skills help a lot on both those jobs." Addy's throat dried up, and her palms sweated.

"We's here at school 'cause our parents make us come. No teacher is gonna make us learn nothing." Red spoke for the trio who nodded their approval.

"Yeah." The solid-built boy with brown hair and a cowlick spoke for the first time. "I don't have to worry about money. My dad is the president of the school board and the bank. I don't need to get a job because he is foreclosing on the whole county." He leaned toward Addy. "Now, Miss Meyers. Don't make the mistake that the other two teachers did. I tell my dad what he needs to hear. Got me?"

"What are your names, young men?" Addy's heart beat in her chest.

Red gave the introduction. "I'm Claude, that's Melvin, and the board president's son is Harry. Don't give us any trouble, and we won't give you any, Miss Meyers."

Addy decided not to press the issue. She didn't want the school board to think she couldn't handle the class. She sized up the three students. The boys stood taller than her. Outweighed her, too. "I'll give you today to sit back and settle in to the school routine. But tomorrow, you need to get to work." The trio smirked in her direction as they relaxed on the bench.

She tiptoed around the room again, inhaling deep breaths. For the first time in a long stretch, her heart spoke for her. *God, help me to know what to do.*

The students sat on benches with a support for their backs. They worked on long tables with a shelf underneath. By the craftsmanship of the furniture, she surmised that parents of the students had built them many years ago. The potbelly stove in the middle of the room told its own story of frigid winter weather. But the promise of a salary to help out Grandpa lightened her step as she surveyed her students' work. Most of the children computed at grade level, especially if they counted on their fingers.

She made a mental note to make flash cards.

For the rest of the day, the students did their seatwork, copying a poem from the board, reading from the McGuffey Reader, and memorizing the Preamble to the Constitution. All with a background of coughing from Katrina.

Addy introduced the Dick and Jane series to the first graders. Everyone participated in learning, except for the trio on the back bench. When her watch read two-thirty, she dismissed the children so they could go home and help with chores.

"Goodbye, Miss, Meyers." Katrina coughed into a handkerchief, then trudged down the lane.

Addy waved a goodbye. "Well, one day down. Thank you, RiverLyn, for helping during math time. Those little ones need a lot of practice to learn their numbers."

"Don't worry. I helped the other teachers too."

"Those eighth grade boys never have to do anything." Billy picked up his lard bucket with a jerk. "Why do I have to do my work if they don't?" He squinted his eyes as he stared at Addy.

"If you want to grow up to be successful at anything, you need to know the three R's." Addy erased the board.

Billy frowned. "Jess makes a living. Don't expect that he has a lot of schoolin'."

"You might be surprised." Addy wiped chalk dust from her desk. "Jess needs to know a lot about math and geometry to dig ditches and spud cellars."

"What's all this talk about spud cellars? Is that what you teach?" A stocky man in a suit knocked on the open door. She recognized him as the person who interviewed her for the job a few days ago. Mr. Hamilton. So this was Harry's father.

"We were just discussing the importance of an education, Mr. Hamilton. What brings you here today?"

"I came to pick up Harry. He's out by the car with his friends. Usually, he will walk to school. Good exercise for the lad. Well, I have come with some rather bad news for you, Miss Meyers. Do you mind if we speak in private?"

Addy nodded to RiverLyn and Billy. They dashed out the door, lard buckets clanking. From the window, she saw them laughing as they played catch with a baseball.

"Seems that the Depression has made its way to our little school here. As the bank president, it has come to my attention that there is no tax money set aside for teachers this year, what with so many ranchers behind in their tax payments. Anyway, the school board has decided you will be paid in script."

A chill laced down Addy's back. "What does that mean, Mr. Hamilton?"

"Well, little missy, don't you fret. A script is a promise that when the county gets enough tax money, it will pay you. Maybe not for a while, but just keep saving your scripts, and one day, you can turn them in for cash. Now, that shouldn't be a problem since you live with your grandpa." Hamilton paused. "Will it, Miss Meyers?"

Yes, it was a problem. A big one. That money was needed for Grandpa to keep the farm. It wasn't fair that her wages were put onto script. How did she lose her salary, just like that?

God, you know how much we need that money. Don't You care?

"That will be fine, Mr. Hamilton. I trust that the county will pay." She said the words that she knew Mr. Hamilton expected, but doubts about the county having any money lingered in her mind.

"Good, good, good. I knew when we hired you that you would be cooperative and not a trouble maker like some teachers we have had. Now, if there is any problem at all with Harry, you let me know. Those other teachers had a hard time with him and his friends, but they didn't know how to handle boys with high intelligence. You come from Topeka. You should know how to challenge smart young men. Well, I must go and tend to bank business."

"Thank you for coming to visit the school."

"Oh, don't worry, Miss Meyers. I'll be back. Believe me, I'll keep an eye on things. Harry's education is very import to the missus and me." Mr. Hamilton chopped his words.

Addy shrunk under the glare of the president of the school board, so grumpy and unrealistic about his son. She clenched her fists when his backside disappeared into the front seat of the roadster. The trio sat in the rumble seat and smiled toothy grins in her direction.

After straightening the tables and benches, she erased the boards and wrote new arithmetic problems in columns for each grade level. She assigned ten problems for the eighth grade students, but they did nothing all day, so her hopes of getting work out of them were slim to none.

If Mr. Hamilton thought the boys were so smart, then why didn't they perform? How could she give them grades on a report card if they didn't do any work? Should she talk to their parents about the boys' attitudes? The problems of last year's teachers zoomed into clear focus. She just couldn't lose her teaching position. Script or no script, it was still a job.

# # #

The sun rose and set two more days on the schoolhouse. Nothing changed within its walls. The younger children worked hard on their lessons. RiverLyn tutored the first graders in arithmetic and reading. The thin, fragile girl, Katrina, coughed in the background all day. Did she have a lingering summer cold?

By the time two-thirty arrived on the fourth day, little light shone through the windows. A dreariness hung over the students like the thick clouds gathering in the sky over the school house. Addy watched as the children mounted their horses and rode off, or walked in groups to their nearby ranches. The graying clouds held no promise of rain, just relief from the blazing sun.

Billy erased the boards. He set to work sweeping the floor when Addy promised to wash and dry the supper dishes later. RiverLyn arranged the reading books while Addy wrote new problems on the board. This time, she did not post any for the eighth grade. Those boys refused to do any work, so there was no point in posting more problems. Instead, she used the space to write the first two verses of a poem for the children to copy in their poetry notebooks. "The Village Blacksmith" by Henry Wadsworth Longfellow, one of Addy's favorite poems that she had memorized as a lonely only child. As they tidied up the school building, a distinct uneasiness overtook her. Gazing out the windows as she shut them, she followed deep gray clouds advancing across the sky like jackrabbits across the desert. The blackness of the clouds and their rapid movements were like nothing she had ever experienced.

Her stomach clenched as she heard the wind blowing. This wind howled, echoing across the empty plains. Low and mournful, it reminded her of the wailing of a wounded coyote, a sound she heard in her bed at her grandparents' house one summer evening. The cry of coyotes sent goosebumps racing up and down her arms, just the way the wind sounded now. For a moment, her body refused to move.

She needed to get Billy and RiverLyn home. Quick! If this storm proved to be a black blizzard, then they faced a danger she couldn't control.

Chapter 4

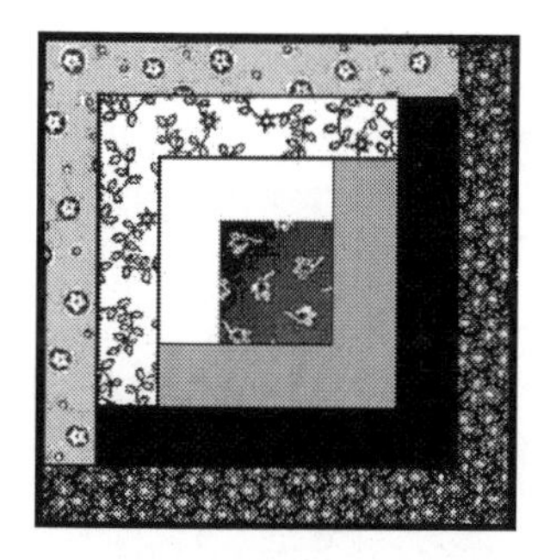

When Jess drove to the site of his irrigation project, Mr. Hulford stood by his dragline.

"One more ditch to finish, and then you'll be ready for spring." Jess drew to his full height as he observed once again his even, straight rows.

"This irrigation system will get those beets growing and ready for harvest." Mr. Hulford hooked his thumbs on his overall straps. "Who knew buying land so close to the Big Thompson River would pay off? I don't have to wait for next year's rain with these ditches."

Jess beamed with satisfaction as he hoisted himself to the cab of the dragline. "Should be finished before suppertime."

"Got to check on my livestock over by the river. Take care, Jess." Mr. Hulford strode across the ditch to his horse that he tethered to a tumbleweed.

Jess turned the key on the dragline and started up the motor one more time. Dig, lay pipe. Then he could collect his wages.

By early afternoon, the sky turned sunless as gray clouds gathered overhead. Not rain clouds, Jess observed, just clouds. Finishing his work on the field, he parked the dragline at the edge of the road and climbed into his pickup. Tomorrow, he'd move the huge machinery. Within minutes, he sped along the dirt road toward Grandpa George's ranch, leaving billows of dust in the tire tracks.

From the mountains, a heavy gust swept across the prairie in an eastward direction. The wind's path followed in the hollows that the furrows had laid in the soil. The irrigated fields boasted straight rows, plowed like the farmers for decades had done. It occurred to him that with no windbreak or strip of unplowed grass land to temper its force, the wind moved along the earth, catching up small grains of sand, shreds of Russian thistles, and tumbleweeds. Farmers said that the soil from Oklahoma and Texas now lay over the cornfields of Illinois and Ohio. Maybe the East Coast as well.

Was that even possible?

As the flat, sandy landscape flashed by, Jess's thoughts turned again to the young school teacher. How was she doing with that unruly bunch of students, especially the son of the school board president? Who also happened to be president of the bank who foreclosed on so many ranchers during the summer.

What was that young man's name? Harry? Jess remembered the boy's distain of anyone who worked with their hands, as he put it. Last spring, Jess dug the irrigation ditches for Harry's father's beet fields, and Harry let him know he was above manual labor. That boy had a lot to learn in life. Addy had a challenge on her hands for sure. Jess pressed on the accelerator.

Glancing in his rear view mirror, he straightened in his seat. He gasped. Behind him, in unrelenting motion, billowed the most gigantic black cloud he had ever seen. The sheer magnitude of it blocked out the sun and extended skyward so high he couldn't see the top. Deciding to outrun it, he gunned the pickup's engine. His heart pounded in his chest in rhythm with the turns of the wheels of the racing vehicle.

That new teacher wouldn't know what to do in this storm.

After speeding to the school house, Jess turned into the horse barn used by the students. He leaped out of the pickup and slammed the huge barn doors shut. He clanked the bolt into place.

The cloud blotted the sun from the sky. Daylight transformed into starless midnight in a solitary second. The black cloud caught up and engulfed him. Jess held up his arms as a shield against the impact of shovelfuls of fine dust flung against his face. He leaned forward, pressing against the biting gravel, groping for the school building's doorstep. The darkness enclosed him so that no light penetrated the swirling murk. He stumbled on the step and felt the door. He gasped for air one last time, pushed against the wooden door, and burst into the school house.

Billy and RiverLyn fought against the whirling wind to shut the door as dust swirled into the room. Addy held a kerosene lamp. He followed the shadowy light to a bench. He sat, struggling to breathe through the fog of dust in the building. Outside, visibility remained near zero. Numberless grains of sands pelted the clapboard siding.

"What is going on? What is this? The black blizzard?" Addy's voice shook.

"This is the black roller that you've heard about. I've been in two other storms like this further south, but not this intense." Jess's shallow breathing punctuated his words.

RiverLyn sobbed. "It's the end of the world. I don't want to die."

Gusts of wind whistled around the corners of the school building and shook the windows.

Jess breathed through his nose. *Stay calm. Keep a level head. Don't panic. A woman and two children are counting on me.*

Addy placed the lamp on the floor, giving the room a shadowy glow. She hugged RiverLyn as the wooden floor vibrated from the whirlwind of dust outside.

"What if the school collapses on us?" RiverLyn asked.

Jess tried to sound confident. "It's just a sand storm. It will be over soon." His statement belied his rising fears. "Good thing the other students had time to get home."

"But it came up so sudden. Just like that." Addy snapped her fingers. "There was total darkness, as though a huge curtain had been drawn around the school house. Such a loud blowing noise. Then the fine dust started seeping in." Addy's voice quivered.

Gritty sand pummeled the panes of the windows as the wind twirled dirt into the air. Billy stepped close to Jess, choking and gagging.

If he could make those sounds, he probably wasn't smothering. Jess patted Billy's back. "Do the children have a kerchief to tie around their mouths?"

"We do. Can't you see?" Addy held the lamp close to her face, which she wrapped in a large white cloth. "Billy, pull your handkerchief over your nose and mouth."

"I heard about cases of dust pneumonia. The fine gravel clogs up the lungs, making it hard to breathe." Jess coughed as he knotted a bandana, covering his nose and mouth. He marveled at Addy's attempts to be calm under these conditions. He had seen many persons cry out in terror or curse during these black blizzards.

Her voice cracked. "I listened as folks told about these dust storms, but in Topeka, we didn't have any like this. How long will this last?" She sneezed several times in a row.

"Just a few minutes more. They don't stick around long in these parts." Jess stared into the wide eyes of the children in the lamp light. He struggled to calm his own racing heart, knowing the dusters he endured further south had been so much fiercer. And some lasted for hours. No need to worry Addy with the reality of the storms.

Please, God, keep us safe in this storm. Hold us in your strong embrace.

# # #

The fence rows held most of the dirt away from the road. Tumbleweeds, blown into the fences, clogged the slats and held back drifts of dirt. Addy had wet some towels in the bucket of drinking water to put over their faces and breathe through as they headed back to the homestead. The pickup needed some adjustments before it started, but now it cruised along the sand-splattered trail, sliding on dust. Jess avoided driving through the sand drifts that did manage to block the road. The sun streaked through a filter of dusty fog. Addy tried to tamp down her feelings.

"No wonder Katrina has dust pneumonia. Her family moved here from further south where the storms are worse. She coughs constantly. I wish that I could help her." Addy's brow creased.

"I've seen my share of cases of dust pneumonia in children. You say that this little girl coughs all day?" Jess's grip on the steering wheel tightened.

"She is thin and sickly. Wants to learn, but it's hard for her to stay focused on her work when she begins coughing. The whole family doesn't look healthy." She remembered a child in Topeka who died of dust pneumonia and a lump formed in her throat.

Jess bit his top lip as he drove through mounds of dirt.

As the pickup wheeled closer to the homestead, the effects of the dust on the landscape lessened.

"The storm must have headed toward the south," Jess observed. "Maybe the beet crop didn't get covered."

She relaxed as much as she could while being squashed in the only seat of a pickup. Her shoulder pressed against his shoulder. The water from the towel cooled her warm cheeks. Billy and RiverLyn huddled close to each other, their eyes still wide with apprehension. Breathing through the wet towels protected their throats and lungs.

"Look! There aren't any chickens!" Billy shouted through the towel as the yard came into view.

When the pickup stopped, he climbed over his sister to get out. He ran to the chicken coop and peeked in. "They're all asleep. They musta thought it was night and went to bed. Don't that beat all." Billy walked back to the pickup.

"Do I hear voices out there?" Grandpa opened the screen door and stepped out onto the dust-covered porch landing. A large, white kerchief covered his nose and mouth, muffling his voice. "How bad was the storm at the school? I was worried about you." He pulled the kerchief down around his neck.

"It was terrible, Grandpa." RiverLyn ran over to hug him. "I thought we was gonna die."

"The schoolhouse took the brunt of the storm. Looks like your spread was on the very edge of it. Not so much dirt piled up here." Jess surveyed the area. "The sugar beets haven't been buried. They may survive this setback."

Addy sighed in relief. Grandpa needed those crops to pay for this land. *Can't lose those sugar beets. Maybe God is having mercy on us, after all.*

"Well, let's go inside and make some gritty sandwiches to eat. We'll all feel better with something in our stomachs." Addy led the way to the door. She removed the towel from her face as the air in the house was dusty, but not as much as in the schoolhouse. Within minutes, they all sat at the table with a plate of peanut butter and jelly sandwiches in the middle.

Grandpa poured milk from a metal container. "Just finished milking Bessie when the storm blew by. 'Bout carried me away when I tried to git from the barn to the house. So dark that I had to feel along the fence to find my way to the back door."

"Let me say grace tonight." Jess paused. "Thank you, God, for all of Your goodness today. For sparing the beet crop. For keeping us safe. For the food on this table. For all of Your gifts, we thank You, Lord. Amen."

Addy never suspected Jess of being religious enough to pray. Maybe just part of his gold-digger act. Even at a young age, she watched men scam her mother. This one wasn't going to turn her into a fool. Life in Topeka taught bitter lessons.

Late afternoon sun beamed through the dusty kitchen air in shafts of flickering light.

The five ate in silence for a few minutes as the hazy air settled. By the time supper ended, a thick film of dust covered everything.

Glancing around the room, Addy sighed. "Okay, kids. Let's use our wet towels to wipe down as much as we can tonight. There will be plenty to do tomorrow, but we can start now to get this dirt under control. Let's begin in the bedrooms. Billy, you clean in your room. RiverLyn, you have ours, and I'll get Grandpa's room."

"Jess and I will go the fields to size up the beets." Grandpa grabbed his hat and the two headed for the screen door.

Addy wet her towel, then walked into her Grandpa's room. She'd avoided going into the small bedroom since Grandma passed on. She didn't believe in ghosts, but the absence of Grandma in the space made it feel hollow. Stepping on the wooden floor over to the dresser, she wiped the surface.

No clutter messed his room. When you didn't own much, you didn't have to care for so much. In some ways, the lack of material possessions made life easier.

She gave the bedframe Grandpa built with his own two hands as a new husband a good wiping. Addy scooped up the patchwork quilt. Passing through the kitchen, she hugged it close to her body. It was almost like having Grandma in her arms. The scent of her homemade lye soap trailed into her nostrils. As she stood on the porch shaking the colorful comforter, an emotion that she could not name fled with the memories and the dust.

When she returned to the bedroom, she spotted a small wooden box peeking from under the bed. She pulled it out and set it on the mattress. She grabbed her towel, and rubbed the layer of dirt from the top. Should she open it? For an instant, she hesitated, but curiosity won out.

She lifted the lid, then stared at its contents. A little white knit cap that a baby might wear. A long yellow nightshirt for a newborn, its string at the bottom tied in a bow. A little boy's knickers made of brown tweed with a small, creamy, white shirt. Who did these belong to? Why had they been folded and kept in a box?

"You found them." RiverLyn stood in the doorway, her dusting towel in one hand. "Please don't throw them away." Her watery eyes sparkled in the light.

Addy gazed at the thin child. "I don't throw away many things, and certainly not something that doesn't even belong to me. Sit down, RiverLyn, right here on the bed with me. Tell me what these clothes are."

"Billy!" RiverLyn called over her shoulder.

Her brother dashed down the hall, the padding of his bare feet slapping the floor boards. "Come and tell Addy about the clothes."

Billy glanced at the box and its contents. He balled his boney hands into fists as he pressed his words through clenched teeth. "You can't get rid of them." Glaring straight into Addy's eyes, he added, "I won't let you."

She drew in a deep breath. She hadn't expected the children's reaction. Although she knew little of Billy and RiverLyn's pasts, she blamed her mother who did not want to have adopted siblings. When her mother refused to let her visit her grandparents, any relationship with the youngsters vanished like a puddle of water in the blazing heat. Grandma's letters filled in some information about the homestead, but not a lot about the family.

"Nobody is throwing anything out. Obviously, these things have great meaning for you. Can you tell me about the babies who wore these garments?" Addy almost whispered. "Do they belong to you?"

"You tell her. You remember it best." A line of tears streaked RiverLyn's cheeks. "Don't leave out nothing, Billy. Tell her all of it. Every bit."

Billy stared into Addy's eyes as he sucked in air and exhaled it through clenched teeth. "People say that kids don't remember things. Well, that ain't true 'cause I remember more than I want to even though I was little when it happened." He shifted his attention to his little sister. "She don't recall anything 'cause she was a baby. But. I. Wasn't."

What could possibly have happened to these children? Obviously it had been traumatic. Even she knew how that felt. Addy's heart beat like a hummingbird's wings. "Please, tell me, Billy. I really want to know."

He stared at the floor. His breathing evened out. He uncurled his tight fists. At first, his voice was almost inaudible. "We come from New York City, Addy. We got a mother and father there. That's why we call our adoptive parents Grandpa and Grandma 'cause we have parents." He stopped talking, and a squeaky cry escaped his lips. Raising his head, he hooded his eyes. "But they don't want RiverLyn and me. They never did."

Addy's heart shattered at his words, and every little piece wanted to scream that she understood his pain. But she sat on the bed as Billy wrung his hands and continued to speak.

"I recollect being hungry. All the time. Never any food. And RiverLyn yelling out for a bottle. Finally, she just whimpered and didn't cry loud like she used to. If I could find food, I would put a bite of bread in her mouth sometimes to get her to stop. Nobody paid much attention to her or to me." Billy shut his eyes as he paused. "I learned early to get out of the way of my father's boots."

Addy struggled to quell the emotions in her heart. They mustn't reach her tear ducts. She almost succeeded. "That must have been hard for you, Billy. What about your mother?"

"She just drank brown stuff from a big mug. Always tired. Too tired to take care of me or RiverLyn. My father and her yelled at each other all the time." Billy twisted the bottom of his shirt with his fingers. The scratch of dust against the house filled the silence. "I hid under the blankets of my bed on the floor. They just let RiverLyn cry and cry. Hardly nobody picked her up or held her. I didn't mind when the men came and took us away. They gave me bread and apples. They fed Riverlyn a lot of milk and wrapped her in a warm blanket." Loosening his twisted shirt, Billy added, "I never slept with both eyes shut until we came here."

Words escaped Addy's mind. There was nothing to say. She fought to keep her composure.

RiverLyn poked Billy's shoulder with her finger. "Tell her about the train ride. Tell her how we was chosen."

"Okay. The men put us on a train car with a bunch of other kids and a woman who called herself Miss Clara. She held RiverLyn close to her. Sometimes she gave her to a big girl to hold or change her diaper. Miss Clara always fed the bottle herself. She told me to sleep, but I stayed next to whoever had my sister. I didn't dare let her out of my sight even for a second. Even to sleep." Billy smiled at RiverLyn who grinned back at him.

"All along the way, the train stopped at towns. Miss Clara made us all get clean and then we stood outside the train. People picked out kids to take home with them. A few times a lady wanted RiverLyn because she was a baby, but didn't want me. I screamed and hung onto my sister's blanket and people always walked away. But Grandpa and Grandma took one look at us and said, 'We want both of them.' That's what they said, so Miss Clara gave us to them and we was adopted."

"How old do you think you were?"

"I was four years old. That's why I remember everything."

"Do you know why they named you RiverLyn?" Did the girl know her story?

RiverLyn's brow furrowed. "No. But, everyone called me baby for a long time until I was adopted. Does my name mean something?"

Addy circled the thin hands of the girl with her own. "I recollect this part of the story, because Grandma wrote me a letter about it. Grandma took one look at your baby face and said, 'This child is precious. As precious as water in a drought.' She thought of a rolling river of water, the sign of a scarce natural resource. So, she named you RiverLyn so you would always know how much you are loved."

RiverLyn encircled Addy's neck in a hug.

"I kept my name. Grandpa said that I can change it if I want, but Billy suits me just fine." Billy nodded toward the box. "These clothes are our New York City clothes. We used them on the train all the way out here. They're what we was wearing before Grandma gave us new ones."

Addy fingered the brown material of the knickers. Then she rose to her feet.

"I'll be right back." Running down the hall, she dashed into her bedroom and opened Grandma's sewing kit. She removed the muslin square and ran back.

"Look." She held it up for Billy and RiverLyn to see. "Grandma made this quilt square from the material she used to sew my graduation dress. This is the Sunbonnet Sue pattern. What is extraordinary is that there is an Overall Sam pattern too."

RiverLyn and Billy viewed Addy through narrowed eyes.

"I just got an idea. How about making a family quilt? I could appliqué a square for each of you using the baby clothes. What do you think of that?" She paused to let them consider the idea.

Billy and RiverLyn cocked their heads and stared into each other's eyes. The answer sounded in one voice. "Okay."

Lifting the garments out of the box, Addy discovered two knitted booties to match the cap. A pair of high top shoes lay on the bottom. Tucked underneath lay a folded piece of thick paper.

"What's that, Addy? I never saw that before." Billy leaned over and pulled out the paper.

The shuffle of work boots from the doorway interrupted her. Grandpa and Jess filled the door frame.

"You didn't see it, because I just put that in there." Grandpa stepped into the room with Jess close to his side. "Now, what are all of you doin' here in my sanctuary? Can't a person have anything private around here?"

"Maybe I should say good night." Jess stepped toward the hall.

"Stay here. You're part of this family, so you might as well know what's going on." Grandpa moved to allow space for Jess in the bedroom.

Since when did Jess become part of this family? I don't even know him. How well does Grandpa really know this man to include him in such private moments? Addy bit her top lip to avoid talking.

"Go ahead, Billy. Unfold the poster and read it." Grandpa sounded calm.

Carefully, Billy unfolded the paper. He cleared his voice, then read.

"'Homes for children wanted. A company of homeless children from the East will arrive at McPherson, Friday, September 15.'" Billy glanced up from the paper poster. "Is that where you got us? McPherson?"

Grandpa nodded. "We took note of the poster nailed outside the general store on a bulletin board. I believe God directed us to go to the train station in McPherson."

"I remember when whole train loads of kids were brought to the farms in Nebraska to help the families there with the farms." Jess smiled at the memory. "It was my job to help find suitable couples for these children, then to monitor their placement. We wanted each one to be successful."

How would a dragline operator be on a committee to find homes for orphans? Who was this man? Addy pressed her questions into her mind for later asking.

Billy cleared his voice again from the dusty air. "Well, here's what it says next. 'These children are of various ages and have been thrown friendless upon the world'. That's true. Me and RiverLyn didn't have a real home."

Jess stepped close to Billy and rubbed the child's shoulder.

Billy read on. "'They come from the Children's Aid Society of New York. Persons takin' these children must be recommended by the local committee and churches.' Is that what you did, Jess?"

Jess shrugged. "In our area of Nebraska, the arrival of the orphan trains required a lot of preparation on the part of the receiving community. Our churches believed that this responsibility should be taken with a serious mind."

"'An address will be given by the agents and the children will be presented. Distribution will take place at the Opera House at ten in the morning.' Were we distributed?" Billy puzzled at the word.

"Sure were." Grandpa nodded.

"So, that's how you knew where to come and git us. Right, Grandpa?" RiverLyn rose to her feet and encircled Grandpa's waist in a hug. He patted her head with his oversized rough hand.

Billy's voice held sadness. "I remember standing by the train and being scared that someone would take my sister away. Why did you want to adopt some kids when your own was grown up anyway?"

All these years, I didn't know about the particulars of these children coming to live with my grandparents. What else did my mother keep from me?

"Grandma and I wanted to have some people around us. We got lonely out here and had a lot of love to spill over onto those who needed it. So, when we went to the train station, we thought we would get some bigger boys who would talk and play Scrabble at night. But when we saw Billy hanging onto that baby blanket and his tear-streaked face, our hearts melted. 'We want both of them.' That's what Grandma said. She fed this little one milk and mashed up food until she plumped out. Thought we'd lose her a few times." Grandpa's eyes glistened. "But Grandma stayed up night after night and got her through. Billy always stayed by his sister's side. You're a good big brother, Billy. Proud of you."

That was the most Addy ever heard her Grandpa say. Grandma always did the talking. A rush of pride swelled Addy's chest as she thought of her grandparent's sacrificial love.

"So many folks just like you and Martha made a difference in the lives of children who needed a second chance at life. Over the years, it was a pleasure to follow up on those orphan train riders and realize how being on a farm with God-fearing people gave them the upbringing they needed to be decent adults." Jess tousled Billy's hair.

Then why are you here? Why did you leave Nebraska? A host of questions niggled Addy's brain.

RiverLyn turned to her. "Tell Grandpa what you want to do with the old clothes."

She held up the Sunbonnet Sue quilt square. "I found this in Grandma's sewing basket. I think it would be fitting to make a family quilt from this pattern of Sunbonnet Sue and Overall Sam. We could use the children's train clothes in two of the squares. Do we have your permission to do that?"

Grandpa searched the faces of his adopted children. "If they want to, I think your grandma would find it very sentimental." He wiped his cheek. "It's good to have you here to help me with the kids. Don't know what I'd do without you."

She gulped. Harry and his friends. Payment in script. Dust storms. Losing the ranch. The problems piled up. How could she help?

Chapter 5

Addy plopped onto the kitchen chair as she wiped damp curls from her neck. She sipped lemonade from a canning jar. Saturday chores were done. RiverLyn joined Addy at the table.

With a soft touch, Addy spread out two muslin squares. "I brought in Grandma's sewing kit. She has sharp scissors and all we need to stitch. Did you ever help her with a quilt?"

"No, but I did some canning with her." RiverLyn shrugged. "Think I can do that again. Mostly, Grandma made our clothes and mended and patched them. All the beds have a quilt, so maybe she figured we didn't need another one."

"Fabric is so expensive to buy. I know she loved picking out feed sacks to get just the right design. She wrote in her letters about the wonderful designs she found at the grain store. Look at that curtain over the pump and sink." Addy pointed to the wash area. "Such pretty green geometric shapes. Grandma had an eye for finding just the right cloth." Addy picked up the paper pattern. "Well, here's the Sunbonnet Sue we are using. Do you have the baby clothes?"

"I took out the seams just like you told me, Addy. Wasn't hard. They was hand-stitched. So, do I just pin it on?" RiverLyn placed the pattern on the yellow baby sack material and used straight pins from Grandma's pin cushion to hold it in place. With care, she cut along the edges of the paper. Taking the Overall Sam pattern, she laid it out and cut along the brown for the overalls, and on the shirt for Overall Sam's undershirt. She cut the hat from the leftover brown material. RiverLyn set the scissors on the table while a satisfied grin brightened her face.

Addy arranged the cut out pieces. "I've got Sunbonnet Sue pinned onto the muslin. Do you know how to make a button hole stitch?"

RiverLyn pressed her eyebrows together.

"Here, watch me." Addy decided to review the stitch. Picking up an already threaded needle, she pressed through from underneath the fabric, followed straight on the folded edge, pushed the needle underneath again, then made a stitch at a right angle to the first one.

"Oh, I remember doing that." RiverLyn regained confidence. "Do I just follow the material around like an edging?"

"That's it. You catch on to working with your hands. Those are skills that will make your life beautiful."

"Just like Grandma did."

They stitched in silence as the sun lowered to the western horizon. Addy couldn't believe the time when Jess, Billy, and Grandpa burst into the kitchen, ready for grub.

"Look. We just finished." RiverLyn held up the Sunbonnet Sue in a yellow dress with a matching bonnet trimmed in Billy's shirt material. Addy laid a square on the table with Overall Sam in brown overalls and a creamy undershirt with a brown hat. She added a hat band from the creamy shirt.

Grandma filled every waking moment of her day with wisdom. Addy wished that her childhood had been filled with the love that her grandparents showed. Deep within, she vowed to do her best to give RiverLyn and Billy the childhood she never had.

# # #

Jess planked his fork on his plate. He swallowed a mouth full of potatoes. "Mighty fine cooking, Addy."

Across the table, heat rose in her cheeks. She twisted the napkin on her lap. "Why, thank you, Jess." Few people complimented her on her cooking abilities. Maybe he had ulterior motives like the men her mother hung around.

"Say it, Billy. You know that you want to, so just say it." RiverLyn elbowed her brother.

"Say what, son?" Grandpa leaned onto the table with both arms.

"Okay." Billy scrunched his face. "I'll say it. Addy, are you listening?"

"Me? Yeah, but wait till I serve this rice pudding." Addy finished scooping the last of it into small bowls. This was one of five recipes she could cook. Gathering up the tray of bowls, she carried them to the table, handing the dessert to each person.

"Thank you, kindly." Jess's words matched the charming smile. Addy stifled the warmth spreading in her chest. She acknowledged his remark with a grin.

RiverLyn hissed. "Go ahead, Billy. Don't be such a baby."

Billy scowled at his little sister. "Well, Addy. We need to talk. Here and now. It won't get no better by pretending it ain't goin' on."

"What? I have no idea what you are talking about." *Please don't bring up what I think you're going to bring up. I just can't take the humiliation. Jess would never understand.* "Did everyone get some cinnamon to sprinkle on top?" Addy reached for the spice jar and held it up. "Makes it taste so yummy."

"Will you let the boy say his piece?" Grandpa didn't touch his dessert.

"What is it that is so important?" Jess's words were garbled by a mouth full of rice pudding.

Billy enunciated every word. "Well, it's about them eighth grade boys."

Addy's stomach clamped together like a bear trap. How could Billy do this?

"Oh, them." Addy forced a high-pitched giggle from her throat. "Those three boys are just too big for those benches they sit on in the back of the room. And we are short one more math book for them." She dared to stare directly into Billy's eyes. "Is that what is disturbing you?" She snapped each word.

"No, Addy. What is disturbing RiverLyn and me and the whole rest of the school is that those boys are doing to you what they did to the other two teachers. They run them off. We're afraid that you will be run off, too." Billy jammed rice pudding into his mouth.

A hush fell over the room so that Addy heard the dust swirl through the screen door onto the kitchen floor. She squirmed under the stares of Grandpa and Jess like spotlights on a G-man's car. "I don't intend on being run off like those other teachers." *I have no choice. I have to teach this class if it kills me. We need the script to save the farm if it isn't too late.*

RiverLyn bowed her head, her words a whisper. "Those other teachers cried during recess. I heard them cry. No teacher should cry."

"Didn't want to tell you, Addy." Billy lowered his voice. "Melvin vowed to get revenge on you for standin' up to them." He pressed his lips as he fixed his gaze on Addy's face. "What those boys say, they do."

Grandpa thumped his fist on the table. "Well, now, exactly what is the problem with the eighth grade boys? Are they causin' trouble like they did last year? Refusin' to work?" Shaking his head, Grandpa leaned forward. "Isn't Harry one of them? He's the son of the school board president. Hmm. That explains a lot. His father is a hard-nosed man."

Sinking onto her wooden chair, Addy decided to come clean. "Those eighth grade boys just won't complete their assignments. They sit on their bench with their arms crossed, glaring at me. Harry says that he'll tell his dad what he wants, and his dad will believe him." *There, I said it. I am a failure as a teacher and everything else that I do. Take that, Mr. Jess, and put it in your hat. It won't be long before I'm fired, and the whole world knows it.* Addy refused to cry, even as her eyes moistened.

Jess's eyes narrowed. "That's intimidation. Bullying." Anger edged his words. "I saw a lot of that in the city where I used to work. There's no place for it in a rural schoolhouse."

"What can I do?" Addy tried not to sound whiney. "If I go after the boys to do their work, then I'll get fired. Isn't it bad enough that I work for script? If I lose this job, what will we do then?" Her cheeks burned. *I'm boxed in with no place to go. If we lose the farm, we'll all be homeless. It happened to my mother. God, don't let it happen again.*

From outside the kitchen screen door, the familiar sounds of the night seeped in. The chickens clucked in their coop, bedding down in their nests. The cows settled the calves in the straw with their gentle moos. Crickets chirped near the well. No one broke the silence of the evening except to spoon in more dessert.

Jess swallowed. He cleared his throat. "You have a secret weapon, Addy. Use it and put those thugs in their place. Don't let them get away with bullying authorities." He laid his elbows on the table.

"Secret weapon? Like the G-men use against mobsters?" Billy liked to listen to Dick Tracey on the battery-powered radio.

"I don't have any power over these boys. All I can do is wait for the grades to come out and fail them." Addy's shoulders slumped. She bit her lip in an attempt to stop an impending flood on her cheeks.

Grandpa sighed. "Now, just listen to me, Addy. You've only come to this homestead recently. We got along just fine for all those years without you. I can handle my finances. All you have to do is figger out a way to git these boys under control. Failing them will set off their parents higher than fireworks on the Fourth of July." He turned to Jess. "Tell us about this secret weapon."

"Well, think about it." Jess leaned on the table, as did everyone else. "According to Grandpa George, Addy was a tomboy. Not only that, but she played sandlot baseball as well as the boys in her Topeka neighborhood. Do I have that right?" Jess winked at her.

"Grandpa." Addy sat straight up in her chair. "Have you been talking about me behind my back?"

"You can play baseball? A girl?" Billy raised his voice and his eyebrows.

RiverLyn slapped Billy's arm. "I'm a girl, and you play catch with me all the time."

"You're my sister. It don't count." Billy scoffed.

"But it does." Jess's voice lowered, and they all huddled close against the table's edge. "I suspect that those eighth grade boys fancy themselves to be hotshot ball players. They haven't seen Billy and RiverLyn throwing or batting, much less catching a baseball. But I have seen both of you in action. Challenge those guys to a game, Addy. If they win, you let them do with they want in class. But if you win—"

"Then they have to work and earn their grades." Determination sloughed off Addy as she straightened up in her chair.

Jess's eyes softened into a brown, like the color of Grandma's morning coffee. *Why haven't I noticed that before? What was he asking her?*

"Do you have a ball and bat somewhere that looks close to official league quality?"

Billy supplied the answer. "There's a ball and bat in the closet. Jonathon's father carved the bat out of a limb of an oak tree he brought with them when they moved here. Silas's mother gathered rubber bands and string to wind around a rock, then his father stitched some pieces of cowhide together to make the ball. They gave it to the school when the last teacher came. I think they hoped that it would help her out at recess."

"We never got to use them." Disappointment edged RiverLyn's voice. "Anyway, I don't know what the secret weapon is."

"The secret weapon is sitting right at this table." Jess pointed at each one. RiverLyn. Billy. Addy. "With the three of you playing ball together, you can have the littlest students on your team and still win. Those troublemakers won't know what happened to them." Jess reached into the middle of the table. "Are you in?"

"In." Billy slapped the top of Jess's hand.

"In." RiverLyn spanked Billy's.

"In." Addy did the same.

"Count me in too." Grandpa folded his calloused fingers and hand on the top of the pile.

Monday morning could not come fast enough.

Chapter 6

As Addy stirred the oatmeal in the iron pot, she reduced the heat from the burner. Billy entered the kitchen, breaking the shaft of dust-filled light streaming in from the window.

"Good." Addy nodded in Billy's direction. "You have on overalls and a shirt. That's what you wear. Nothing suspicious."

"I have on my rubber-soled shoes. They help me dig into the sand and run better. Those bullies aren't going to know what hit them today." Billy popped a piece of toast into his mouth.

"Do I pass the innocent test?" With pigtails and a pink-checked dress, RiverLyn oozed femininity. Not the look of a tomboy. Only her shoes hinted she might want to break out into a fast run. Addy knew by playing "running bases" with these two that their looks hid the truth of their talent.

"Perfect, RiverLyn. You don't look like you could throw a ball, much less catch one. However, I have had the advantage of watching you two practice baseball skills and know how well you perform. Even if we do not win the game today, we will give those big lugs a show they will never forget." Addy dished up the oatmeal as Grandpa entered in the kitchen door.

"That Dettmann feller is a real go-getter. He's up at the crack of dawn with that dragline of his. Spud cellars, he told me. For farmers putting up harvests this fall. With land being on the edge of what they call the Dust Bowl, a lot of the homesteaders are puttin' up potatoes." Grandpa plopped onto a wooden chair and scooted close to the table. Addy placed a bowl of steaming food in front of him.

Giddiness worked its way from Addy's chest to her lips, distracting her from the task at hand. Why did Grandpa keep bringing Jess into the conversation? She just noticed the biscuits burning on the bottoms in time to salvage them.

Billy spooned some brown sugar onto his oatmeal. "I haven't never seen Jess at church. Does he go to church, Grandpa?"

"Now, don't you go worryin' none 'bout things that don't concern you. I know for a fact that Jess worships in an honest way that most folks in this town wouldn't even know about. He spent a bit of time talkin' with Martha 'bout church. But, that's confidential information. Ask Jess yourself if you have a question that is dyin' to be answered." Grandpa poured coffee into his pottery mug. "Let's say grace for what we got. The Lord has supplied us above and beyond what others around here have. RiverLyn, how 'bout you do the honors?"

RiverLyn bowed her head while folding her hands. "Dear Jesus, thank you that we have enough food to eat. I know other kids whose stomachs growl at school, so I want to be grateful. Help us to play ball the best we know. Amen."

Addy peeked at RiverLyn while she prayed. The child always reminded Addy of a picture of cherubs she had seen years ago. Innocent. Pure. Vulnerable.

Grandpa shooed Addy, Billy, and RiverLyn away from the kitchen sink and onto the path to school. As they sunk into the dust on the gravel road, Addy realized how much sand shifted places in the landscape because of the storm. Piles of soil lay in drifts along the south side of the slatted fences that served as wind breaks. Tumbleweeds rolled everywhere in the gentle wind, bringing movement to a lifeless scene. Once-flat land now waved with small piles of dust. When the trio arrived at school, Addy inhaled a deep breath and smiled. The area around the school house had been raked flat.

As she stepped into the building, her heart pounded. "Look, kids. The parents must have come and cleaned the classroom. Just a thin layer of silt on everything. Let's dust it all off before the students get here." Addy handed cloths to the children, and they went right to work.

She glanced around. "The dust will settle in no time, but this is a welcome sight after the storm."

She heard Katrina before she tiptoed into the classroom. Her persistent cough was raspier, sharper than last week. More frequent too. Katrina's mother held her hand.

"I hope you do not mind. My family came here yesterday to be sure things were clean for Katrina. She has dust pneumonia, you know. The doctor tells me she will be better here in the northeastern part of Colorado. Where we lived in Oklahoma, she was much sicker."

Dust pneumonia. Children died from it. Old people, too. The dirt clogged the lungs until the person could no longer breathe and suffocation resulted. Should Katrina stay in school?

"What should I do?" Helplessness almost overwhelmed Addy.

"Just treat her like any other child, but don't expect her to be active." The dress sewn from flour-sack material hung on Katrina's mother just like the shirt on Grandpa's scarecrow flopping in the breeze. "She is improving all the time. The storm set her back a bit, but she will recover. Pa and me are staying with his folks until he finds some work. We just drove the horse and wagon here a month ago, and Katrina has gotten some color in her cheeks already."

Where? Those are pale white cheeks. *Dear God, help me. I am not prepared for all of this.*

'Didn't mean to move in on you, Miss Meyers. Now, study hard, Katrina. I'll meet you at the end of the lane after school." With a kiss on her forehead, Katrina's mother left the child standing by the entrance.

"Please, come in and take your seat."

Within minutes, the buzz of excited students filled the schoolhouse. Addy turned to start the pledge when a hush fell over the room. The tramping of boots behind her signaled the arrival of the eighth grade boys. She stepped to the front of the class to take charge before they did.

"Rise for the Pledge of Allegiance, please." Everyone stood with their hands over their hearts. For some reason, the eighth grade boys had never given grief about being patriotic. "Let us recite the Lord's Prayer to start the day." Again, the whole class joined in the prayer. Addy peeked to make sure. *The opening exercises do not offend these fellows. Just the teacher and the work. It's personal.* The clue to their behavior did not help her cope with it.

Katrina coughed. She covered her mouth with a man's large, white handkerchief. The wracking of her shoulders caused Addy to flinch.

"This morning, we will start with our grading groups." As she gave directions, she knew without looking that the back row of boys now slouched on their seat, ready to spend a day doing nothing. She gritted her teeth. Glancing over at a young child, she commented, "Good work, Jonathan. You have all your words written down and your dictionary open."

Several children sat up with their backs straighter, and Addy smiled at each one.

A snicker from the back of the room broke the silence. She chose to ignore it.

Sitting in her teacher chair, she gathered the first graders around her. She introduced them to the word look written on a piece of tag board. She instructed the children to look and make a riddle out of something they saw. The children enjoyed the game. Finally, they read the word in Dick and Jane book, while talking about the picture above the word.

Addy assigned them to erase their slates, then write the word look ten times, saying the letters as they printed. Katrina punctuated her efforts with coughs. Maybe the chalk dust was causing some of her problems. Addy would try to get her paper and pencil to work with rather than a slate.

The morning dragged on. Yawns, squirming on benches, and chuckles from the back row interrupted the work of the other students. She sensed the younger students' underlying uneasiness as she had the first day of school. Today, she needed to settle once and for all how the rest of the year would proceed. With her or without her. She repressed the thoughts of losing her job and the promised script. *God knows how much I need this job, but He also knows how much I need to control this class.*

The autumn sun hung like a blazing ball high overhead at noon. Hot, dry.

Perfect.

Addy moved into the plan.

Sashaying to the back of the room, she reached the trio of eighth grade boys. "Well, young men." Her voice lowered as she leaned in. They met her halfway across the table. "I see that no slates were written upon. No spelling words memorized. No books read. No numbers calculated. Am I right so far?"

Claude shook his red hair. A snarkle flew from his nose, to the amusement of Melvin and Harry. "Oh, you are so right." He turned his head to wink at his coconspirators.

"Well, I think we should settle our differences of opinion once and for all. Today. Everything or nothing. Are you up to the challenge?" Maintaining a genuine smile, Addy tried to quell the fluttering in her stomach. The shuffling feet of children with pent up energy blended with the soft coughing of Katrina in the background.

The three straightened on the bench and glanced at one another. As leader, Claude spoke. "We can take anything you dish out, Miss Meyers. But, I don't believe that you can take us much longer. Two other teachers who were older and tougher than you didn't last a year. What makes you think that you can?"

Grandpa's farm. Two thousand dollars in script. Honor. Fortitude. Obviously, there was a badge of honor among ruffians that included humiliating teachers

She slowly drew in a lungful of breath. *Now, think before you speak. God, if You are there, give me the words I need.*

"In the best interests of all involved, it is important that I teach this classroom of students with no problems. Your parents are expecting you to learn the curriculum for the eighth grade. If I cannot do that, then I will step down and let the school board hire someone who can."

She paused for effect, holding their interest. "So, I challenge you to an all-American baseball game. You win, I go. If I win, you behave and work." The Regulator clock ticked as the idea sank into their heads. "What do you say?" She quivered as she realized how much of a huckster she became to do this. Like all those slimy con artists that took her mother's money. But the importance of her mission overrode any second thoughts that surfaced on her conscience.

Claude turned his head and eyeballed Addy with suspicion. Melvin and Harry raised their brows in surprise, then Melvin nudged Claude and nodded his head. Harry's smirk told a story of overconfidence.

"Who has first pick of teams?" Melvin's voice shook.

"You, of course." Addy played her part. "After lunch?"

The boys huddled together, and whispered. When they finished, Claude extended his hand. "Deal."

Addy shook his hand. "You betcha."

Her affirmation sealed the deal.

# # #

The sun shone high over the mountains as it paced itself to the overhead position when Jess could pull out his lard bucket with the lunch Grandpa George packed at the crack of first light. Martha always made some sandwiches for him, and even an oatmeal cookie with raisins for a treat.

Yes, God watched over him as he headed out West over a year ago and brought him to George and Martha's homestead. Their delight in his simple acts of digging a spud cellar, creating an irrigation ditch system from the tributaries of the Big Thompson River, and helping plant the beets brought him immense satisfaction. After years of working hard and feeling frustrated, being part of this little family stirred emotions that he didn't even know existed.

That Addy. She was young and spunky as they came. If she set her mind to something, then it was done in the time a jackrabbit clears an open field. Those boys at school better watch their manners. Maybe he and Grandpa George could straighten them out if the baseball didn't work.

Switching off the ignition, Jess stopped digging the Henzleman's spud cellar for a moment to drink some water from a Ball canning jar. Silence from the roar of the dragline's motor filled him with much needed solitude. He eased himself off the machine, then walked over to his sack of supplies. As he looked up to let the water slide down his dusty throat, movement caught his attention. A man climbed to the top of a rock and dusted the dirt off his hat and shoes. His dry lips pressed together.

"Need a drink of water?" Jess called out. The visor on his hat shaded Jess's eyes as he took in the details of the man's appearance.

"Don't mind if I do," the stranger answered. Within minutes, the space between the men closed.

Jess handed a full Ball jar of water to the lanky man. "You sure are a long ways from civilization. What kind of business do you have way out here?"

Not a hobo. Stubble shows a recent shave. Shirt is from the same shop I used to buy mine, and that isn't cheap. Slacks are sturdy for this kind of country. Boots show wear of being broken in for many a mile. Camera on a strap around his neck. Taking pictures for Prohibitioners? Illegal booze running?

"Name is Arthur Rothstein." Art held out his hand and shook Jess's. "I work for the FSA, Farm Security Administration. Government issued, you could say." He chuckled.

"Jess Dettmann. Spud cellar digger. Irrigation specialist." Jess patted the iron wheels on his dragline. Poofs of dust clouded the air.

Arthur held up his camera. "Photographer. Who ever thought I could get paid to do what I love. Taking pictures provides me an opportunity to travel all over the West. Glad to finally be in a part of Colorado where there is water and a bit of agriculture." He unscrewed the lid and drank from the canning jar.

"With the Big Thompson River and the ability to irrigate, these homesteaders can raise a few crops. I know that the dust storms we experience here don't hold a candle to those black blizzards farther south." Jess paused. "I think I detect an Eastern accent. Where are you from?"

"New York City. The Bronx. I know. This is a big change from the tenements. I even had to learn to drive a car to get this job." He nodded toward the Model T Ford parked along a row of tumbleweeds.

"Hate to be nosey, but why are you snapping pictures?" *Correction. I need to be nosey. This fellow wouldn't be the first huckster to pass through this area and take advantage of folks.*

"The government wants a group of us photographers to document what this nation is facing during the drought. Especially out in the West. Someone coined the term Dust Bowl, and it sure fits this mess. With the photos we've been taking and sending back to Washington DC, the experts may be motivated to think of something to do to help those poor people in Oklahoma."

"What parts have you seen?" Jess squinted as visual images raced through his mind. *I saw plenty of suffering on my way from Nebraska to here.*

Arthur took another swig, licking every drop of water from his lips. "I came West in '33, so it's been several years of wandering around Texas and the Oklahoma panhandle. The worst I saw was when I arrived in Boise City, Oklahoma. Nothing but dust everywhere, and black blizzards for hours or even days, raging till people lost their minds. Went to a lot of funerals for dust pneumonia, both young and old." Art's brown eyes darkened like a rolling thunder cloud. He smoothed back his straight, brown hair.

Jess stared at Arthur for a moment. His gut told him he could trust this stranger. A rare thing in this part of the country. "Same kinds of conditions that drove the people into the Hooverville over in the foothills. Have you had a chance to go there?"

"Not yet. Be obliged if you went and made some introductions. Sometimes those folks don't like outsiders like me." Arthur chuckled.

"We can go this weekend, if you want. Have you gotten any photos that tell the suffering of the people in this long drought? Politicians out East really don't understand how bad it is."

"Funny you should bring that up. I was out on a homestead in Cimmaron County, Oklahoma. The Art Coble place. Nothing but dust for miles in every direction. Hard to believe that farm raised crops eight years ago. Took pictures of drifts of sand so big that they almost buried houses. I was about to get back into my car when I turned around to wave to Coble and his two sons." Arthur paused while the sounds of wind moving gravel grated in the background.

"I looked back at Coble, and what I saw was this man bending into the wind, with one of the boys in front of him and another behind him. Great swirls of sand all around made the sky and earth blend into one. And I said, 'What a picture that is.' I just picked up my camera and clicked. One photograph. One shot. One negative. Never again will this happen." A satisfied grin upturned the sun-browned, dry skin of Arthur's young face.

"I saw that picture in the Omaha newspaper just before coming out here. Really made people sit up and take notice of the suffering of the farmers who sit on nothing but sand." Jess's heart beat hard with his recalling of the iconic photo that sparked conversations in Omaha.

"Made the Feds start to realize what's happening. All of our pictures are telling a story that is scaring President Roosevelt into action. I hear that some Civilian Conservation Corps men were deployed to Oklahoma to try some new farming techniques and plant some wind breaks."

Jess sighed. "Anything they can do will be a welcomed change. After all, it has been eight years of hardship. Maybe '38 will be a year when things turn around a bit."

"Do I know you from somewhere? Your face seems to be familiar." Arthur leaned forward to peer at Jess.

"Don't think so. Got a common looking moniker here. Just a dragline operator." Jess pulled the visor of his hat lower over his eyes to shade the contours of his cheeks. He turned away from Arthur's gaze.

"I've seen and met so many people, I probably have you confused with someone else. Well, I'm staying in town at the boarding house, and if I don't get there on time, I won't get any grub. House rules. It would mean a lot to go to Hooverville before I head out." Arthur handed the canning jar to Jess. "Thanks for the water."

"I'll be in touch." Jess walked away to place the water jars by the sack. *That was too close for comfort. The last thing I need is for someone to recognize me. Addy knows nothing of my past.*

Taking his hat off, Jess wiped the sweat from his brow.

Chapter 7

The sun cast short shadows as the students sat on the steps of the school building. Pulling the lids from their metal lard buckets, a variety of lunches filled the fingers of hungry children. Jam dripped on homemade buns. Corn bread with black strap molasses spread thick in the middle. Thin tortillas wrapped around an assortment of vegetables. The trading of tastes was a long-held, time-honored tradition at this school. Addy watched as the swapping took place. Nothing changed at lunch time, no matter where or what decade.

Most students carried jars of milk, now quite warm with a thick head of cream on top. Rings of white circled the first graders' lips. Because nobody brought much to eat, it didn't take long for the munching part of lunch recess to pass. Now, for the play time.

"Okay, class. Gather round." Addy waved her arms, then checked to make sure her hair was still pinned into a bun.

"What are we doing, Miss Meyers?" Jonathan piled his lard bucket on top of the others already stacked in the large woven basket.

Katrina coughed into her hand. Dark circles under her eyes highlighted her condition. Addy creased her brow before she spoke.

"Well, there are eighteen students and one teacher. That makes nineteen people. But, we need an audience and score keeper. The first graders make up the cheering section, and our only second grader, Clara, shall be the score keeper. Katrina, will you help Clara?"

The two girls stepped toward each other. Katrina coughed again.

"Are you all right? Do you want to go home?" Addy asked.

Katrina shook her head.

"You and Clara sit here on the steps. Use a stick to make a mark in the sand for every home run, Clara."

"I can do this, Miss Meyers. Come on, Katrina. Let's go sit." Clara's pigtails bounced as she clasped Katrina's hand. The girls smoothed their feed-sack dresses as they sat on the wooden entrance to the school.

"What are the rest of us going to do?" Merle glanced at Billy.

"We are going to have a baseball game. Just for the fun of it. Right, boys?"

"We look forward to the chance to play." Harry bowed.

"Merle, Billy. Go to the hall closet and get the ball and bat." Addy thought for a moment. "What can we use for bases?"

"There are some empty feed sacks over in the horse's shed." Jonathan started walking in the direction of the low lying lean-to. "Want me to get them?"

Addy nodded. "Those will do just fine."

"Fill them with straw." Claude pointed at Jonathan, who nodded that he heard.

Billy and Merle bounded from the school house. "We got 'em." Billy held up the bat and Merle held up the leather wrapped ball. Addy marveled at the accuracy of the home made objects and the love the parents invested in these items for their children. Finally, the sports equipment would be used.

"Okay. Let's see." Addy heard Katrina cough and kept up her mental count of the child's difficulties. "Well, how about Claude be the captain of one team, and Billy be the captain of the other. Claude, you're older. You choose first."

So far, so good.

"Melvin." With a swagger, Melvin moved alongside Claude.

"I want Addy, I mean Miss Meyers." Billy's cheeks reddened.

Claude nodded toward Harry. "Harry."

Billy smiled. "RiverLyn." As she tiptoed over to Billy's side, the skirt on her pink checked dress swished with the wind. The eighth graders laughed so hard they held their stomachs and sides.

Oh, RiverLyn. You are a scamp. Perfect. They'll never know what hit them.

When he regained his composure, Claude chose a seventh grader and two six grade boys. Billy teamed up with Jonathan, Merle, and a third grader, Lillian. The rest of the class sat on the entrance stoop, right behind home plate.

"We bat first." Claude grabbed the bat and strolled over to the brown burlap bag which served as home plate. Billy took the pitcher's mound, which was a square drawn in the dirt with the toe of his foot. RiverLyn danced like a ballerina over to first base, much to the jeers of the older boys.

Don't overplay our hand, RiverLyn. Everyone keep a cool head in this hot sun.

Addy ran to the outfield while Merle and Jonathan covered second and third bases. Bookworm, a tiny girl with straggly thin brown hair, stood behind Claude as the home base catcher.

The audience yelled, "Play ball!" Anticipation hung in the air as heavy as dust clouds.

As she dashed to the outfield, Addy picked up her pace, enjoying the freedom that running always allowed her as a child. Pent up in an apartment with a sullen mother waiting for a tipsy father figure, she savored her time in the vacant lots playing ball with the neighborhood boys. They taught her how to slide into a base, how to catch without a mitt because nobody owned such a luxurious object, and how to tag. Most of all, she gained the confidence she needed to face obstacles. Just from those sandlot games in Topeka.

Turning to face the school house, she anchored her feet in the dirt, standing nose to nose with the biggest challenge of her life. Putting her job on the line might not have been the best idea, but desperate times called for desperate measures.

"Batter up!" she called out. *Show me what you've got.*

The shorter sixth grade boy, Tim, sauntered to home plate with a loose swing of the bat from his hand. Addy didn't notice the firm biceps on the twelve-year-old before. Sweat beaded on her forehead as the sun blazed down.

Tim let Billy's high pitch swish by. Lillian, the skinny catcher, fumbled the makeshift sphere. She threw the ball back with an underhanded throw like in a game of horseshoes. Merle groaned as he crouched behind second base.

Billy pulled back his arm and let the ball fly right in the strike zone. Tim connected the bat with the leather and took off for first base. He touched the burlap bag filled with straw a second before Billy landed on the pitcher's mound. Staring at Tim, Billy held the ball until Tim settled on first.

Charles, the other sixth grader, strode to the bag and picked up the bat. A lefty. Billy struck him out in three well-executed pitches. Claude glared at Billy while Harry told Charles to go sit with the girls. Tim stayed planted on first, but he leaned on his knee as he readied for the next hit.

Harry grabbed the bat, then tapped it on the ground with every step. Hovering over home plate like a falcon over roadkill, Harry turned to Bookworm. He snarled, "You'll be eating my dust."

Lillian back-stepped.

"Come on, Billy! Show me what you've got." Harry gripped the wood with white knuckles.

Billy drew back and delivered a fast ball. Crack! The ball sailed into the air as Tim raced for second, then third. Harry ran over first and started for second. Addy raised her hands to cup the ball. When the leather smacked her fingers, they stung. The ball fell into the dust as the crowd on the school steps went wild. Tim pumped his legs to home plate. Lillian backed off the burlap. Seconds later, Harry slid onto the bag with both feet, hands overhead. The big boys hooted their excitement at the homer.

"Two runs for Claude's team." Clara shouted above the voices. Katrina coughed under the din.

The seventh grader, Will, strutted to home plate. A studious young man, he worked with his parents in the fields before and after school as well as all summer. Strength and agility blended in his athletic body. He preferred to be alone. He didn't follow the big boys, but didn't oppose them, either. Shielding his eyes from the sun as he spotted Billy, he clutched the bat.

Lillian pounded her right fist into the palm of her hand and squinted.

Billy threw two low balls to Will before he lobbed one right into the strike zone. Will put all his force into the hit that sailed high over Billy's reach and into the outfield. Addy ran to meet it on the first bounce. Picking up the ball, she threw it to third base where Jonathan caught it with a smack to his bare hands. Will hunkered over the second base burlap bag.

Clara yelled, "One out! Two runs!" The kids on the steps squirmed.

Claude and Harry clapped Melvin on his back before he made his way to home plate. His lower lip jutted out as he faced Billy. Will swayed in anticipation of running to third.

Billy drew back and let the ball fly. Harry swung and missed.

"Strike one!" Clara screamed.

"Shut up over there if you know what's good for you!" Harry countered.

Lillian chased the ball and underhanded it back to Billy.

For several moments, Billy and Melvin locked gazes. Then Billy moved into his baseball pitching stance that Addy watched every day when he practiced with RiverLyn. With one flowing motion, he set the ball on course right where Melvin hit, which sent the ball right to where

Addy stood. She focused on the incoming sphere, and caught it in a tight grip. Her fingers stung.

Will slipped onto third with a thud.

Addy sent the ball to first, and Merle lobbed it to RiverLyn. Pulling back, RiverLyn whipped it to Billy faster than the boys could register. When Billy held up the ball, the eighth grade boys' jaws dropped. Their reaction did not escape Addy's notice.

"You're out!" Clara jumped up and down. "Two outs!"

The heat is on Claude, now. Let's see how he reacts under pressure. *Maybe I'll discover what is underneath all that defiance.* Addy's legs moved back and forth like a boxer's as she held down the outfield. Sweat slid down the back of her neck. Her bun loosened, allowing tendrils of hair to hang. Pounding her right fist into the left hand, Addy commanded, "Batter up!"

Claude stomped to the hitting mound, leaving footprints in the dust.

# # #

Jess heard the automobile engine heading toward him. He turned to see Arthur's car which left just a few minutes before.

Leaning out the window, Arthur yelled. "Hey, Jess. When would you like to go to Hooverville? Soon?"

"I could manage to go today if you want. Give me a minute to secure this site. Working in the heat of the day has never appealed to me." This job would wait until tomorrow. Putting the keys to the dragline in his pocket, Jess grabbed his sack of empty Mason jars and stowed them in his pickup. "Your car or my truck?"

"I need the practice driving. Hop in." Arthur ground the ignition several times before the motor turned over.

Jess glanced into the back seat. "Looks like you have a grub stake back there."

Arthur chuckled. "Got a sleeping bag, an ax to chop tree limbs, one shovel to dig my car out of the dirt, a water bag, and a Coleman stove. Not bad camping gear for a city boy."

"Not bad at all."

With all the windows in the auto rolled down, a hot breeze blew on Jess's face. Fine dust sanded his exposed skin. A blue sky with no clouds topped the mountains as they traveled westward into the foothills.

Jess leaned out the window when the car raced by the lane that led to the school yard. Shielding his eyes from the sun, he spotted a bunch of kids out on the flat dirt.

So, the ball game was in session. That spunky little teacher sure needed to win this game over those bullies. Guess he wasn't the only one who had to stand up against intimidation. He gave Addy credit for having fortitude. She didn't back down easily. Jess grinned as the car disappeared behind a snow fence lined with tumbleweeds. He liked that kind of quality in a woman.

"Tell me more about your work." Jess bounced in his seat as the tires hit bumps in the roadbed.

Arthur held the steering wheel with one hand and leaned on his elbow that tanned outside the car's frame. "I work for the Farm Security Administration as a photographer. I'm in contact with Dorthea Lange and Russell Lee. We're documenting all of the misery that people are experiencing across this nation. The soup kitchens, long lines of men seeking work in factories, and the hobos as they ride the rails. Actually, most hobos I met were once men who held responsible jobs at one time but can't find another. Even met Woody Guthrie at a train station."

Jess glanced over at Arthur. "Isn't he the feller who is writing songs and playing his guitar?"

"He is. Hitching trains to California to support the unions so the fruit pickers can earn a decent wage."

"What did you see in Oklahoma? They got hit the worst from what we all hear."

A serious tone marked Arthur's words. "People who have had the life beat out of them. Some call them 'Next Year People' because they are always jawing about how next year it will rain, or next year it will be better, or next year the crops will grow. But things just keep getting worse and worse. This drought has been going on for too long."

"How can they make it from day to day?" Jess thought of the families in Hooverville just around the bend. Men and women who just a few years earlier were independent ranchers.

"It's hard. Those farmers sold everything of value to buy food. Barely enough to eat on a given day. Sometimes the government sends them some flour or other surplus food. More than coping with the hunger, the worst thing was hearing someone cough."

"Dust pneumonia. I've had to officiate at some funerals of children who died from it. Don't know how the parents carry on. Makes a grown man examine his faith when little ones pass on." Jess's voice hitched on his last words. How many times can a man stand over a casket with the sounds of Fanny Crosby's hymn, "Safe in the Arms of Jesus", being sung?

"I've had a lot of time on this job to examine my beliefs." Arthur swerved to miss a pile of dirt on the road. "My family is Jewish. Being in Cimarron County pressed the story of Moses leading his people in the wilderness for forty years into reality for me. Only difference is that Oklahoma has wild dust storms. And there is no daily manna for those farmers like the people of Israel enjoyed."

Jess allowed the roadbed to provide sound as he considered Arthur's words. God promised His faithfulness day by day. Moment by moment. But so many people didn't have any mercy in their hard lives. Did God know the suffering of His people? Did He care? Would injustice just keep piling higher with no sign of let-up?

Jess pointed to a small stand of trees. "Park the car under the shade. It's a short walk."

They took a few steps before a pleasant voice greeted them. "Preacher. What brings you around here in the middle of the week?"

"Preacher?" Arthur formed the word with his lips. He lifted his eyebrows.

"Calvin. I want you to meet Arthur Rothstein. As you can see," Jess indicated the camera hanging around Arthur's neck, "he is a photographer. Works for the government. Can he take some pictures of Hooverville?"

"If it gets the feds movin' on recovery, then take all the film you need to get the job done."

Arthur held out his hand and Calvin clasped it. "Glad to meet you, Calvin. Now, tell me how you got to this Hooverville. You know there are hundreds of these makeshift cities all over the country."

Jess noticed how Arthur paid attention when Calvin spoke. How he leaned in as if Calvin's words mattered. The men walked as they talked.

"Well, Arthur. Three years ago, the missus and I had a ranch right here in Colorado. Two hundred head of cattle at our peak. We rotated the open range areas for our cattle's feed and had three ranch hands to help. Those cowboys did a good job, but with no rain, all the grass just dried up. The cattle starved. The saddest day of my life came when the feds shot my herd, giving me pennies on the pound. We lost everything when the bank foreclosed." Stopping in front of a small wooden shack, he called out. "Got some company."

A thin door comprised of two orange crate sides nailed together squeaked on iron hinges. A smiling but gaunt woman with brown hair pulled into a tight bun stepped outside. "Who's with the preacher?"

Jess. I'm just Jess. Don't look at me that way, Arthur.

"Arthur, this is the missus." Calvin put his arm around her shoulder. "This man wants to take pictures of the camp. Can you take him around and introduce him to the children and such?"

"Sure will. Come along, Arthur. Now, let me show you where we cook some of our famous soups." The two headed for an iron pot hanging over a campfire. Several women with babies sat on logs nearby. The murmur of Arthur's calm voice blended with the background sounds of a hundred people moving about with daily chores.

"Let's be serious, Calvin. How are things going here? Are you getting set for the winter?" Jess tried not to think about a Colorado snowstorm in an uninsulated wooden shack. Or a tent. Or the lean-to constructed from wood, cardboard and pasted-on newspapers. Or the fact that families lived in these hovels. *Dear God, help these people survive.*

"We were talkin' as a group last night. Most of us want to head out to California at the end of October. A few have folks in Arkansas. They can make it there with a bit of God's grace." Calvin tried to sound optimistic, but Jess had known him long enough to read the signs of despondency. "We all just need to git a bit of cash for the gas. Prayin' that some odd jobs come in."

"Let me pray with you right now." Jess laid his hand on Calvin's shoulder. "Heavenly Father, You know the pain that this man carries as he heads this group of people. Supply their needs as they prepare to go to a warm place for the winter. Help them to be healthy and safe when they get there. Give Calvin here the confidence he needs in Your great love. Amen"

"Thanks, Preacher. Some days the load is just too much. Now, where do ya suppose that Arthur fellow is?"

The noise of children talking and laughing drew them to Arthur, who took photos of the children as they played marbles, sat on boulders, or gazed into the future. The snap of his shutter ticked off the hours of the afternoon onto rolls of unexposed film as he chronicled mothers holding babies while sitting on bent-birch chairs.

By the time the sun glazed the mountains with a red glow, Arthur's shoulders drooped as he drove his car back to Jess's dragline. Each man rode without speaking as clouds of dirt flew from the tires. Arthur pulled up close to where Jess's pickup was parked.

"How do those people keep on going? Why don't they just give up? What can we do to help them?" Arthur's eyes brimmed with tears that he brushed away.

Jess allowed the silence to cloak them for several minutes before speaking in low tones. "Are you serious about helping?"

"Never been more serious in all my life." Arthur stopped the vehicle. He fingered the camera strap lying against his shoulder.

"Addy has a student with dust pneumonia. If we could get her family to a relocation camp in Washington, the little girl's breathing would improve. They need transportation. Going that way soon?"

"I'll work it into my schedule." Arthur smiled. "Thanks for taking me to Hooverville. This is just what DC needs to see. I'll be in town for a bit longer. Then I'll go to Yakima, Washington, to photograph that resettlement camp. Look me up when the arrangements are made with the family."

"I will." Jess waved good-bye to Arthur as he headed toward town. Jess slid into the driver's seat of his pickup. Tumbleweed followed him all the way back to the homestead.

The scent of home-made biscuits wafted from the kitchen's screen door. Jess filled his nostrils with the smells of home. Hearth. Family. A deep longing stirred in his heart. Exhaling, he knocked on the screen door before entering.

"You're just in time for biscuits and gravy. My favorite supper." Grandpa George carried a pot of coffee over from the stove. Pouring a mug full of the steaming brew, he handed it to Jess before placing the enamel pot on the table. "Pull up a chair. I see you washed up at the pump."

"Thanks, Grandpa George." Jess blew across the top of the mug before he sipped. He watched Addy lift the fluffy biscuits from the cookie sheet with a spatula and place them on a large plate. His mouth watered.

"Bless this food that was given from Your hand for this day. Amen."

"Your prayer is always short and to the point. No wonder Grandma loved you so much." Addy passed the gravy.

Jess placed his napkin on his lap. "Well, I'm dying to know how the game turned out."

Chapter 8

RiverLyn jiggled in her seat while Billy buttered his biscuit. "Hurry up and tell Jess." She pointed her butter knife at her brother. "Or I will."

Billy jumped right in. "You should have seen it, Jess. Claude's team had two outs, and Claude went up to bat. He was stomping mad, which was just where I wanted him. I had saved up my special pitch just for him."

"Oh, he was fit to be tied because his team only had two runs." RiverLyn stopped talking to stuff her mouth with a creamy piece of biscuit.

"Billy played it all so casual that nobody knew what he was up to. Except RiverLyn and me." Addy cheeks flushed with excitement.

Billy chuckled. "Claude kept callin' out to me, tryin' to make me unbalanced."

RiverLyn kept the pace going. "But, he couldn't. Even when he yelled 'that's girl-throw pitching', Billy paid him no mind."

Addy cut in. "Then Billy, cool as a cucumber fresh out of a tank of well water, says, 'Here's my heater.' He leans back, raises his arm, checks RiverLyn on first base. He steps into the swing. When I saw the snap of his wrist and the release of the ball, I knew that Claude would strike out. One, two three. He went down so fast he couldn't get any madder."

"So, how did your team do?" Grandpa heard the story as soon as Billy and RiverLyn burst through the screen door, but Addy knew he wanted Jess to get all the details fresh from their mouths.

"Well, Lillian was first up to bat, which was good because she struck out right away. That put a grin on those big boys' faces." Billy reached for another biscuit.

"Yeah, and a secret grin on ours." RiverLyn chuckled.

"Merle and Jonathan both got on base. Then Billy tapped the ball on the bat and landed on first. The bases were loaded, and no runs. Claude, Harry, and Melvin just about laughed themselves silly when RiverLyn in her pink dress tiptoed to the home plate." Addy allowed the happiness to spill over into her hands as she gestured.

"Oh, you really played it up, didn't you? It must have been a sight to behold." Jess's eyes twinkled in the light from the kerosene lantern in the middle of the table. His smile warmed Addy's cheeks. How could this man make her feel so giddy inside?

"Oh, RiverLyn really took some chances." Addy picked up her fork and stabbed a hunk of pickled beets.

"I knew exactly what I was doing. That Harry can't pitch anything but fast balls. When you're that predictable, it takes the fun out of it, but makes it easier to play off." RiverLyn's eyes sparkled.

Billy's voice grew louder with each word. "She missed the first pitch with a girl swing, you know, real weak. Then she whacked at the second fast ball that Harry sent dead over the plate."

RiverLyn choked with laughter. "By then, Claude and Melvin were yelling, 'Batter, batter, batter', thinking they were so funny."

Jess swallowed. "Did that unnerve you any?"

"Naaaaah."

"Then RiverLyn took her real batting stance." Addy paused. "That snapped everyone to attention. Harry looked confused, but he threw his best pitch. The bat connected with the ball, and it sailed high in the air. Merle slid into home plate, with Jonathan, Billy, and this pink streak right behind. Claude fumbled the ball when it smacked his hands, but threw it to home plate too late for Melvin to catch. It almost hit the scorekeepers."

"Clara really went into action. 'Four runs for Billy. Two for Claude.' She musta said that ten times." Billy slapped his knees.

"How did the big boys react?" Jess took another draught of his coffee. Addy caught his gaze and held it long enough to read the warmth in those java-brown eyes.

"They were fit to be tied, and yelled at each other. All the little kids cheered. It was something!" Billy and RiverLyn talked at one time, then they grinned at each other.

Billy sat straight with a wide smile spread across his face. "I saved the best for the last, Jess."

Jess's eyebrows arched. "How so?"

Addy tightened her lips as her cheeks warmed.

"Well, only Addy didn't bat yet. Everyone knew that she had to either strike out or get on base. They started to get back to their old selves again as Addy took the pins out of her hair. 'Easy out!' they yelled. 'She's no Dizzy Dean.'" Billy allowed a dramatic pause to heighten his story. "Those kids were shocked when she bent her knees and followed through on the ball. It flew so fast they didn't even see it zip by their heads and land in tumbleweeds way past them. Addy sped over those bases like a jackrabbit being chased by a coyote. By the dumb expressions on their faces, I knew the game was all over." Billy clasped his hands over his head in a victory stance.

Grandpa chuckled. "Well, that should settle down some of those problems in that school. I knew ya had it in ya to meet the challenge, Addy. Now, how about you kids clear the table and help me with the dishes?"

# # #

While Billy and RiverLyn groaned about cleaning, Addy and Jess stepped onto the landing outside to breathe the evening air.

"So, what did you do today?" She stared at the first stars of the night.

"Started out with a spud cellar, but ended with an interesting afternoon." Jess told her of his encounter with Arthur and their visit to Hooverville. "I was thinking about that little girl in your class when I drove back here. The one with dust pneumonia."

The images of other children clouded his mind and bothered his soul. "Maybe the family could ride with Arthur to Yakima to the resettlement camp. Better air to breathe, and a job picking fruit for the father. It's temporary, but healthier than here. I know several families whose loved ones got better when they got out of Omaha." He paused. "Too many children died of dust pneumonia. Those are the hardest funerals to attend. The parents are devastated. I can't stand by and watch another youngster succumb to the disease."

"Katrina's mother will bring her to school tomorrow. I'll talk with her and see what we can do. Katrina is coughing quite a bit. She needs a change."

This woman genuinely cared for her students. Jess moved toward Addy, touching his arm against hers, feeling the warmth of her body. Compassion in all this misery was a rare commodity.

"Tomorrow, I'll finish the spud cellar that I started today. I'm considering going along with Arthur and bring back some of the apples from Washington. The folks at Hooverville need some fresh fruit. So does Grandpa George. Apparently, the Northwest is experiencing a bumper crop of apples. So many that train cars filled with fruit arrive on the East coast so men can sell apples on street corners and make money."

"Sounds like a plan. If you get enough, I could try my hand at canning applesauce for the winter." Her offer to store food melted Jess's heart. He longed to work with a woman to build a home and a future.

She leaned on Jess's chest as he folded her into his embrace with a contented sigh. The sky darkened around them, stars twinkled overhead, the chickens' clucks faded.

He wanted to believe that life could be just like this moment in time, so filled with happiness. But reality usually crowded in and set him straight. No, this was just a moment. One. Moment.

# # #

The next morning, Addy and Jess both greeted Katrina's mother as she led a thin, boney horse with Katrina riding bare back. Jess helped the child down, then exchanged pleasantries with her mother. He watched as Addy held the girl by her hand and led her to the school building. Katrina waved good-bye to her mother.

Jess heard the child cough, and glimpsed her large, white handkerchief. Several students scrambled through the entrance with their lard bucket lunch pails clanking as they bumped the doorposts. The horse neighed and pawed the dirt.

Finally, Jess got down to business. "I have an offer for you and your husband. A photographer is driving to Yakima, Washington, in a day or so to document the resettlement camp there. There is room for you in his car. I can follow along with some of your luggage and supplies in my truck. He says that the resettlement camp is fairly basic in its housing, but there are lots of jobs picking apples and other produce."

"My husband and I need work. We can harvest fruit. Is there is a school for the children of the laborers?"

Jess's voice softened. "Yes, there is a teacher for all eight grades, and a doctor who comes once a week. The air in the Northwest is clear and free from dust. It is what your daughter needs if she is to get well."

If it's not too late, he wanted to add.

Katrina's mother walked the thin horse down the path. Jess kept pace.

"Can you come and speak with my husband? We could work for a while, save our money, then come back here and help out the folks. You're right. The farther we get from this dry, dusty place, the easier it'll be for Katrina to breathe. Have you ever seen a child die from dust pneumonia?"

Jess nodded. "Too many times. Too many times. For a while, I conducted two or three funerals a week for children after I watched them slowly suffocate on dust." He knew he could not sing "Whispering Hope" one more time without totally breaking down.

After setting up the trip with Katrina's parents, Jess drove out to his dragline and finished digging the spud cellar. Somehow, the energy from knowing that Katrina was getting help propelled him in his work. Exact corners, ninety degrees. Proper depth. Straight walls. No wonder some of the other machine workers called him "Micrometer Eye".

He heard the motor from Arthur's car. He turned. The vehicle spewed a dust cloud as he drove down the gravel road. The good news burst out of Jess as soon as Arthur stepped from the auto.

Arthur clapped Jess on his back. "That will be a life-saving trip for that little girl. Glad that you can go along and bring their things. The tents and shacks that the fruit growers provide are empty. They will need some basic household goods to take with them."

"No problem. I always wanted to go to that area of the country at this time of the year. Want to bring back some apples for the people in Hooverville." Jess's lips watered just thinking about the applesauce Addy wanted to can for the winter.

Arthur leaned against the dragline wheel. "Well, if we can get started tomorrow morning, then we will be in Washington in two days. Think that can be arranged?"

"I'll get right on that. Want to meet at Grandpa George's farm?"

"Sounds like a plan. By the way, Reverend Dettmann, I remember why you look so familiar. Your picture emblazoned every Omaha newspaper for almost a week. Front page the first time. Then the copy hit pages three and four."

Jess cringed. No matter how much he tried, his past encroached on his present like a bear caught in a steel trap. "I suppose the truth wouldn't make a difference to anyone."

"I already know the truth. Followed the debate you had with the church board because it interested me. Coming from New York City, I never heard of a pastor taking on his whole board in such a public way."

"When my own congregation is part of an ongoing problem, then I have to do something. It took a lot of prayer on my side to get to the place where I confronted half the elders and deacons. Believe me, it was not a situation that I took on without thinking of the consequences." Jess refused to apologize for his actions. Then and now.

"Never thought I'd meet you out here, but I need to say that I admire your stance. When grown men agree to adopt unfortunate children from New York City, then they need to follow up on the terms of that agreement. You blew the whistle on their behavior. No wonder those men were angry."

"Orphan train riders. That's what they call those young men that the deacons and elders lined up to get when the agents came to Omaha. I was young and naïve, and those rich men on the ministry board all got me to sign as their pastor that they were capable of adopting these homeless waifs. You had to see these kids standing on the train platform, Arthur. Scared, acting tough, needing love. That's what I thought these men in my church would do. Treat them like sons. Raise them with compassion."

Arthur shook his head. "We heard that some people just wanted the older boys for indentured servants. That is not what the Children's Aid

Society promised to these young men. They were told families would take them in."

Jess was impressed at how much Arthur knew and understood. "When I told the agents from the Children's Aid Society how the young men were expected to work hard on farms or in businesses but never build up a herd of cattle or put away money, then the agents moved the orphans to families where a second chance at life was possible."

"I can imagine that the church members were not happy about that."

"The ministry board made life miserable for me until I decided to resign. Who would have guessed the newspapers would pick up on such a story? And twist the facts to make it sound like I took children away from decent homes?"

Jess's shoulders hunched as he hung his head. Addy did not need to know this about him. How could she ever love someone who failed so miserably in their calling in life?

"Personally, I admire you for standing up for those who cannot speak for themselves. It takes courage, Jess. More than most men have."

"Only Grandpa George and his wife know my story. I'd appreciate it if this information just stayed between us. No one else needs to be told about my past until I've sorted it out."

Chapter 9

"Tell me again. You're going where? For how long?" Addy crossed her arms against her chest. Anxiety riddled her body. Everyone she counted upon always left her.

"Just for a week." Jess dug the dust with the toe of his boot.

"But what if you break down? How will you get help in the middle of nowhere?"

"I have mechanical skills, and I'll put some tools and extra tires in the pickup."

"What about dust storms? What if you get caught in one?"

"Been in dust storms. Will be able to handle it."

Addy shifted the weight of her body to her other foot. "Katrina will have problems with the dust."

"She's having problems now. This is the best option that this family has."

Maybe I don't want you to go. Her heart raced. "I understand, but I don't like the details of the trip." She liked the way that Jess looked in the opening rays of morning.

She scurried to fix enough cornmeal mush for the crowd she expected at any moment. The rooster crowed into the silence of dawn. Shards of sunlight streaked from the mountain tops, breaking into the coolness of the morning.

"RiverLyn, get those bowls and spoons set out. We want it all ready when they come."

"Katrina is really going all the way to Washington?" RiverLyn placed one of Grandma's best silver plated spoons beside the hand-crafted pottery bowls. "Will she get better?"

"Jess says that it is the only way to keep her alive. The dust settled in her lungs. She can't keep inhaling the air around here." Addy tried not to replay her conversation with Jess. No man ever made her so vulnerable.

"It's going to help Katrina if her father gets some work." Placing a pitcher of fresh milk on the table, RiverLyn inspected her work. "Grandma would be glad you're using her silver service. It's the one thing she owned that she said was elegant."

Addy stirred the mush one more time. "Katrina's family needs to be treated with kindness and compassion. They lost everything in the dusters when they lived on the Oklahoma panhandle. It has been hard for them to take charity." She set a small pitcher of molasses on a saucer before placing it on the table.

"I hear them coming. Billy! Where are you?" RiverLyn bolted out the screen door. "Oh, you and Grandpa are out here waiting."

Addy checked the table, with two leaves in it, one more time. An embroidered table cloth from her Grandmother's starched stack of linen graced the table. What would she have said? "It's not what you own, but how you make others feel that counts in life. Use your best to make others feel better." Well, this is how Grandma Martha would have welcomed Katrina's family.

Everyone trooped into the kitchen and found a place at the table under Grandpa's direction. Katrina coughed into a handkerchief as her mother cupped her shoulders. The father shook hands with Grandpa and chitchatted with him. Jess filled the door frame with his muscular body. Hesitating for a moment to remove his cloth hat, he returned Addy's glance with his endearing, crooked smile. As Jess moved into the room, another man followed him. A young man. Addy's age. And handsome.

A slow blush crept from her neck to warm her cheeks.

Grandpa pointed to empty chairs for Jess and his guest. A camera hung by a leather strap from Arthur's neck. The two men sat down as she brought the bowl of corn meal mush to the table. The only open chair for her was between Grandpa and the stranger. Addy squeezed into the place, conscious of the man's nearness.

"Let's hold hands for our blessing this mornin'." Grandpa grasped Addy's, his rough and weathered palm against her fingers. Arthur's clasp, however, was warm and soft.

"Dear God, we come at this sunrise with thankful hearts for this fine food you've afforded us. Bless Jess and Arthur as they take this family to a place of healing and hope. Be with them every step of their journey. Amen." Grandpa squeezed Addy's fingertips.

"So, who is this young man at our table, Jess? I see he's brought a camera with him." Grandpa poured some coffee from the pot into his mug.

Jess gestured toward Arthur. "This is Arthur Rothstein. He's employed by the Farm Security Administration and has gone all over the Dust Bowl photographing what's happened to the farmers. These pictures are changing some of Roosevelt's policies."

Addy scooped corn meal mush into each bowl as she served her guests. Billy got the pitcher of milk started around, then the molasses chaser. As she stood by Jess to ladle his portion, she breathed in his earthy scent. How she loved the smell of the land. The natural, organic connection with life.

Arthur thanked her as she placed the golden grain in his bowl. "This is the kind of breakfast that satisfies the stomach and the soul. Grits and corn meal mush. Living can't get better than this." His upturned lips salivated as he stirred in the molasses.

Only the smothered coughs from Katrina interrupted the focused eaters.

"We have a long trip in front of us. Are you all set?" Jess addressed Katrina's parents, who nodded as they finished eating.

Katrina's mother twisted a handkerchief with her fingers. "I'm so nervous about all of this." Her brow settled into deep creases.

"Why?" Addy breathed the word.

"What if the trip is too much for Katrina to handle? What if we get to Yakima and there is no work?"

"There are no guarantees in life. My grandmother would say we need to trust the Lord for our steps. This must be difficult for you." Addy relied on her grandmother's words, not her own experience.

"It is. We have nothing in worldly goods. All we have is Katrina. It is not easy to have faith."

"I know. That I do know." Addy held the mother's boney frame close to her for a moment.

Grandpa patted a canvas bag as he handed it to Katrina's father. "I baked a loaf of bread last night for you to take. Put some honeycomb in there to sweeten it. Billy and I will pump some cold water into canning jars for you to take." With a nod, Billy joined him outside by the windmill.

Addy observed Arthur as he stepped to the door, and watched as the water containers were placed into the back seat of the car. RiverLyn slid past him and tossed a baseball to Billy. As she crouched for a catch, Arthur snapped her athletic pose. The shutter closed on Billy as he made a long throw to Jess. Addy framed the pictures in her mind and saw what Arthur might have seen. Children growing up in difficult times with normal reactions and responses to fun.

Katrina's coughs drew Addy back into the kitchen. Grandpa walked in to help the little girl to the door, while the parents lugged several canvas bags of food from Grandpa. Addy squatted until she was eye-level with the child.

"Katrina, you are going to a state where the air is clear and the water is pure. A place where your lungs can heal. Keep studying your speller and read the McGuffey book I lent you."

"Don't worry, Miss Meyers. My mother made a poultice of onions and mustard and laid it on my chest. I won't cough up a bunch of gunk if I wear it." Katrina's lips formed a weak smile.

Hopelessness overwhelmed Addy as she realized that the child coughed up mud.

As Addy held the tiny hands and stared into Katrina's brown eyes, the camera snapped. Arthur documented their moment. She glanced into Arthur's eyes and read the compassion in them.

Arthur posed Jess and the family in front of the pickup with all their belongings. "Usually, I take photos of families who are in despair as they leave the known for the unknown. As hard as your journey will be, there is hope at the end of your ride." He focused his camera as they smiled. He took several pictures of the lean family dressed in clothes sewn from feed sacks.

In one way, it was an invasion of their privacy. But the outside world needed to know how bad it was here on the Great Plains. Thank goodness for Arthur and the others who were trying to capture these poignant moments of time.

Jess moved to Addy's side. "I expect to bring back some apples for the folks at Hooverville and for Grandpa George. I'll miss your cooking while I'm away." His eyes twinkled. "Hope those fellers at school learned a valuable lesson. They have a good teacher."

He squeezed her shoulder. She lowered her eyes as she bid him safe journey.

Just before climbing into the driver's seat, Arthur strode over to Grandpa and shook his hand. "Thank you, sir, for all you have done to help today. And for taking care of Jess." He tipped his hat to Addy and the children, then moved behind the steering wheel of his sedan.

Arthur's remark sparked questions in her. What did he mean by that? Taking care of Jess? Why?

Within minutes, she watched as Arthur drove the family in his sedan, and Jess followed the dust trail in his pickup loaded with all the belongings of Katrina and her family. When the vehicles drove out of sight, heaviness settled in her heart. She missed Jess. She missed his off centered smile, his casual way of speaking, his down-to-earth logic about everything.

The sun crept just above the mountain tops as Addy, Billy, and RiverLyn trudged to school. The walk there cleared Addy of all thoughts of Jess as she focused on the challenges that faced her when she arrived. She received no feedback from the parents of the three eighth graders, and she expected the worst when they found out what kind of agreement she made with their sons. What sort of teacher had she become?

Addy got the board work chalked in just before the students arrived. Today, she included substantial work for the eighth graders. It was a test to see if she resolved the power struggle with her students.

The children entered in silence, placing their lard buckets in a row before sitting on their benches. An air of expectancy hung over them, and Addy squirmed a bit as she handed out chalk and slates. Just as the Regulator clock struck nine o'clock, the three teens sauntered through the door. They shuffled as they moved to their bench in the back and slouched onto it.

Her heart sank. What made her think that anything would change? That she could keep this teaching job and help pay off the taxes? Tears threatened to squeeze from her eyes, but she held them back by biting her bottom lip.

"Rise for the Pledge of Allegiance." Addy braced for the day of humiliation she faced.

One by one, the younger students rose to their feet and placed their hands over their hearts. The bench in the back creaked. She peeked over her shoulder. Claude, Harry, and Melvin stood straight with their hands pressed on their shirts right over their hearts. Never had the pledge sounded so sweet to her ears. She wished Jess was in the room to see this change. He would be proud.

The morning clock ticked the moments as the students flowed from one activity to another like water from the well's spigot. RiverLyn kept the first graders on track with their addition and spelling. Addy read with several groups before she turned her attention to the eighth graders in the back. Standing as tall as possible, she strode to the back of the room to face her fear. Sweat pearled down her back.

She had no back-up plan if the boys refused to complete their assignments.

Harry spoke up first. "I worked out the math problems from the board on my slate, but my calculations don't agree with Melvin or Claude on several of them. My father is the bank president. He expects my sums to be exact. Last night he told me to get ready to start helping him on Saturdays with the books. I need to be able to do this, or he'll give me a strapping."

Claude shook his head. "I don't know if mine are right or maybe Melvin's is right. My dad needs help with the sacks of feed he sells at the store. I know he thinks I can add all this in my head, but I can't." His brows crossed.

Glancing over at Melvin, Addy asked him, "How are you doing?" He stared at the table in reply.

She relaxed her shoulders. All those years of giving the teachers a hard time finally caught up with these boys and now they hit crisis mode. She longed to tell them that they deserved what they got but knew that would not be productive. A mind ready to learn is a precious thing. And finally this trio was ready. She got to work.

The clock gonged twelve times. The deficits in their learning included a slow recall of basic math facts, an incomplete understanding of place value, and a lack of ability to solve equations with variables. Her work, and theirs, was cut out for them for the rest of the year.

As she sat on the school entrance with her jelly sandwich, chatting with Lillian, the three teens slumped on the steps beside her. Lillian made a hasty retreat to a group of children congregated near a large tumbleweed.

"Where did you learn to play ball like that?" Harry bit into a baking powder biscuit.

"Yeah. Girls can't throw a ball. But you can." Melvin nodded.

Claude drank milk from a canning jar, then wiped the white foam from his lips with his sleeve. "You sure surprised us. We didn't think you had it in you, but you did."

"I grew up in Topeka, Kansas. Lots of boys in the area, and they needed one more for a team. I was the only other kid available, so they drilled me every day on basic skills until I was one of them. Best time in my life." Addy meant that.

Harry stared at her for a moment. "Most teachers are all fluffy and scared of snakes and bugs and everything. They sure don't know how to play ball. You're different, Miss Meyers. That duster didn't make you move back to Kansas. Maybe you can give us the learning we need."

"I hope we have a good year together. We all need to find success." She took a swig of Grandpa's well water from her Mason jar. Jess was right about gaining respect from the boys by proving she had some grit in her. He was annoyingly right.

The afternoon flew by so fast that Mr. Hamilton caught her by surprise when he stood in the door frame at three o'clock.

"I came to pick up Harry. He is going to start an apprenticeship at the bank. I hope he has his skills all up to date, Miss Meyers."

The panic in Harry's face told its own story.

"We are working on all he'll need for his grade school diploma. Aren't we, Harry?"

Time to get a commitment.

"Absolutely, Father. Miss Meyers is the best teacher I've ever had." Harry smirked a bit, but his friends' faces remained expressionless.

"Well, let's get going. Time is money." Mr. Hamilton shut the door on their quick exit.

The rest of the class got their lard buckets and headed home on foot, horse, or wagon. Within fifteen minutes, Addy, RiverLyn, and Billy trudged back to the homestead for the weekend.

# # #

On Saturday morning, Addy woke up early from anticipation. She expected to accomplish a lot.

Taking out her grandmother's sewing basket, she laid out on the kitchen table the three quilt squares she and RiverLyn had completed. Today, she hoped to add to that number. Digging into the small stash of fabric remnants, she spotted a scrap of blue and white striped material from a shirt that Grandma made for Grandpa. Brown tweed from the cut-off cuffs of a pair of dress pants. Tracing the Overall Sam pattern, she created a figure that reminded her of the city-like sophistication of Arthur. A tan hat with a blue-and-white hat band completed the square. Taking a patch of gray silk, she appliquéd a reasonable facsimile of a camera. A few embroidery stitches produced the details on the camera and created a strap just like Arthur used to carry his equipment. As she pulled the last stitch, satisfaction settled on her like a hen covering her brood of eggs.

She thought about the young photographer as she created the Overall Sam design. Arthur Rothstein and all the others documenting the Dust Bowl represented the effort being made to help sort out what had happened to so many ranchers and farmers since the drought started. When she still lived in Kansas, the Topeka newspaper printed a few of the photos, and the emotional impact of those images of families living in despair haunted her.

Grandpa suffered like everyone else on the Great Plains, but his homestead drew irrigation water from mountain rivers. Access to water separated those who survived from the ones whose crops and livestock dried up. Now, the bank wanted to foreclose on Grandpa.

It was all about the water.

The thought unsettled Addy.

Maybe the issue of water explained Jess's diligence in digging irrigation ditches for Grandpa's beet crop. Although older than herself,

Jess exuded youth with maturity. A combination that her mother never met in a man. Yet, here he was. An intelligent worker who helped Grandpa create a way for cash flow that the president of the bank, Harry Harrison, coveted. Addy didn't like the way her logic led her thoughts. Better to think about happy memories.

Her mind centered on Grandma. A woman with the dried skin of a person who spent a lot of time outdoors in the garden, with the hens, helping with livestock. The scent of yeast bread clung to her. Her eyes sparkled from the devotional time spent with her Bible on the porch. Grandma's voice exuded her assurance in God's faithfulness, so there was no need to fear the future.

But Addy feared so many things. She wished she had Grandma's faith.

Taking each remnant piece from the sewing basket, Addy realized most were from the feed bags that held the chicken's grain. Geometrics, stripes, flowers, any color. Grandma must have made a lot of aprons, tops, curtains, and quilts from the textured fabrics. At last, she lifted up a piece of feed bag material left over from an apron she remembered Grandma wearing as she puttered around the kitchen making flapjacks that she smothered with molasses. Touching the tiny blue and yellow flowers on the grainy material pressed a tear in Addy's eye. This would make a perfect dress.

On the bottom of the scrap pile, she found a light yellow fabric just the right size for Sunbonnet Sue's smock. A square from a solid blue grain bag that was large enough for the bonnet lay under a green plaid. Shoes. Socks. There were enough little odds and ends of material to create a Sunbonnet Sue Grandma. With great care, Addy cut and stitched the design onto the white feed bag background.

"What're ya doin', Addy?" Grandpa stood behind her, staring at the shapes on the table.

"Still making the quilt. Got two more squares finished. One for Grandma."

Grandpa blinked, his eyes watery.

"And one for Arthur. His work intrigues me. By the way, when Arthur left, he said that you cared for Jess. What did he mean?" she tapped the bottom of the chair next to her as a signal that she and Grandpa needed a long talk.

With his arthritic bones creaking, he sunk onto the chair. "Might as well tell you the whole story." He rubbed his chin, then nodded his head. "About a year ago, we heard some talk from friends in Nebraska that a young preacher was in trouble with the elders and deacons in his church."

"That was Jess?"

"Reverend Dettmann," Grandpa corrected. "Only been preachin' at this influential church for a year, but they wanted him gone."

"What did he do that got them all riled up?" She couldn't believe that someone as calm and logical as Jess made enemies.

"While Jess was in theology school, he served on several committees that helped to find homes for kids who rode the orphan trains. He was on the board that cleared your grandma and me to get RiverLyn and Billy. Was serious about his task. Stayed in touch with the boys that he placed, and found that some of them weren't gittin' what the agreement said they should git. From wealthy families."

"That's not right. How could people do that?" Addy's narrowed her eyes.

"When Jess became pastor of the Omaha church, he preached against greed and such. The worst offenders toward the orphans were some of the elders. They made life miserable for him, and he quit."

She didn't know any ministers, but the thought of them stepping down from the pulpit puzzled her. "Quit the ministry?"

"Took his money and bought a dragline. Started diggin' ditches and roads. We heard he needed a place to stay and invited him here. He's been livin' in the log cabin ever since. Your grandma put in a lot of time to help him heal his heart toward people. She had a lovin' way that was like a balm to the soul."

"And Arthur knew about this?"

"Anyone who stands up for justice and speaks for those who have no voice will get noticed. Jess's picture was in the paper a couple of times. Arthur remembered seein' the articles and asked me if that was Jess. But I warned Arthur not to talk about it. Jess jest wants to live his life in a quiet way."

She allowed this news to settle in her brain and her heart. Jess knew about bullies and intimidation from personal experience. No wonder he wanted her to stand up to the eighth graders.

Grandpa leaned closer to Addy. His eyes sparkled. "Jess is a fine young man. You won't find none better than him for moral courage and work ethic. A smart girl sets her cap for such a man."

"Grandpa! I am not setting any cap for anyone. It takes all my effort just to teach each day. And we need to get this beet crop harvested. I hope you haven't forgotten about the money we owe."

"Don't you worry about the money. That's my department." Grandpa's eyes lost their sparkle.

"Does Mr. Hamilton want this land because it has access to water?"

"That is the only thing Hamilton wants. Water rights are the biggest reason for range wars here in the west. Since Jess dug the irrigation system for me, Hamilton has been salivating like a rabid dog. He can't wait to get the deed to my land. If I die trying to stop him, then that's what I'll have to do."

"What's the plan?"

"Don't have a plan. Just harvest the beets, and trust the Lord that the sugar refinery pays cash."

Her heart sank. Maybe Grandpa didn't have an organized plan, but Mr. Hamilton did. The bank president orchestrated the paying of her salary as script.

Chapter 10

Jess hung his left arm out the pickup's window as he clutched the steering wheel with his right. He longed for a deep drink of well water and some home cooking.

Piles of dirt in wind-shaped dunes dotted the desolate landscape, the effects of the Dust Bowl winds. To the west, the Rocky Mountains climbed to the clouds, with rivers rushing water to the hungry irrigation ditches sliced in the earth. The herds of scraggly beef that survived on tough vegetation wandered listlessly on the sand. Soon, the only signs of life were connected to the mountains, the rivers, or the irrigation ditches. As far as Jess's eyes could see, dry sand laid waiting for a duster to stir it up.

The shadows of evening spread over the homestead when Jess pulled in with his load of apples. Billy ran out of the kitchen door, letting it slam behind him.

"Jess! Jess! You came back. It's been a long time." Billy let Jess mess up his hair. "Look at all them apples. They sure smell good."

"Take some into the house to be washed. They are delicious right now." Jess's legs tightened when he walked, and his back ached from driving. He needed to brush his teeth and soak in a long, hot bath.

Grandpa opened the door. "Got some corn bread and navy bean soup." Billy ran by him with an armful of fruit. "Those are mighty good looking apples."

"Sure are. They travel well. Hope to get them to Hooverville tomorrow so the folks can eat them at their prime." Jess moved over to the sink and pumped some water into a basin to wash the dirt off his arms and face. A towel hung on a hook over the sink. He dried his eyes and then opened them.

Addy stood across the room, pushing her hair behind her ears. A warmth flowed from his feet to the top of his head as his heart beat as fast as a jackrabbit's back foot thumping on a log.

"What was it like in Washington? Will Katrina like her new home?" RiverLyn bit into an apple with a slurpy bite.

"Each family who works in the orchards has a solid-built one room cabin. It isn't much, but it beats the Hooverville style. Still lots of poverty in the Yakima resettlement camp. Hard to get ahead."

"Did Katrina stop coughing?" RiverLyn talked with her mouth full.

"It will be a long recovery, but the air is clean, and her mother got every speck of dirt from their new home. The women in the camp all helped."

"What about Arthur? What was he doing?" Grandpa asked.

"Taking pictures of the camp. Women washing clothes. Men picking apples. Children studying in a makeshift tent. His camera snapped all the time." Jess chuckled at his memory.

Glancing at the bushels of apples, Addy sighed. "Well, guess we'll be trying out that community canning center tomorrow. Good thing it's

Saturday. I did tell you I wanted to make some applesauce, didn't I?" She sat beside the only empty chair. Jess plopped down beside her.

"I used to help my folks with the canning. But it's been a long time since I was involved in such a project." Jess handed his bowl to Billy for a fill-up of soup. "Guess it will all come back to me."

Grandpa George cleared his throat. "Let's say grace. Thank you Father, for travel mercies for Jess. Bless this food. We're mighty happy to get the apples. Amen."

"Amen." Those at the table agreed.

Jess allowed the comfort of home to embrace him for a few moments. But his logical mind told him not to let his heart run away with him, because Addy didn't know his secret. If she did, there was no way she would want to move in the direction that he wanted.

# # #

Addy bustled around the table, sweeping up after breakfast. Some of the kitchen tasks became second nature to her. Maybe this was how Grandma managed to make this ranch into a home.

"Okay, Addy. Help me get today's itinerary straight." Jess dried the morning's dishes as Grandpa washed them in an enamel basin. RiverLyn put them away.

"Well, we go to the general store in town and get some feed for the chickens. It will take a few minutes while I pick out material for the backing of the quilt. Then, we take the apples to Hooverville. On the way back, we'll stop in town for the afternoon to can a bushel."

Addy lifted a box. "Billy, put these canning jars and rings and lids in the truck. I'll get some sugar and Grandma's canning directions for applesauce." She scurried around the kitchen as she spoke. A quiver inside kept her feet and fingers moving. She and Jess would spend a day alone.

Before long, they bounced in the pick-up on the way to town. The wind from the window blew her hair into her face. She kept pushing her tresses over her ears. She relaxed as she angled her arm out the window. "So, Katrina is settled in?"

"The resettlement camp is where displaced people can get a grip on life and then re-enter the work force. Right now, getting that little girl's lungs cleaned out is the prime focus of the family. I think the state of Washington may offer some ways for them to get back on their feet. This economic downturn has left so many couples scrambling to put food on their tables. It is demoralizing to most men who want to be breadwinners and providers."

"Grandpa is fortunate to have a cash crop and water. It kept him in a place where he can at least try to hang onto his land. Do you think the beets will bring in enough money?"

"Just a few more days, and then the harvest starts. If the soil under the beets is moist and they can be picked at one time for the sugar refinery, then he has a chance of paying off the bank loan. I suspect he'll make some money for supplies for the winter as well."

"I hope to turn in my script and then have money to give to Grandpa to help care for all of us. I like teaching, but doing it for free is not paying the bills."

"It's a matter of faith. God has our lives in His hands. He knows how much we can endure."

Did He? Fear gnawed at Addy in the most surprising places and times. She was afraid of failing as a teacher. Afraid that Grandpa would lose the farm. Afraid that she couldn't be the sister-mother image that RiverLyn and Billy needed. Afraid that she'd fall in love and the man would end up like her mother's failed relationships. Faith? She doubted she even had any. What did Grandpa say? "Everything you dream about is on the other side of your fears."

She stared at the general store as Jess parked the pick-up. So many people getting supplies on this Saturday. The placed buzzed with the sounds of mothers scolding children and men discussing the prices of grain, gas, and flour. The scent of fresh-harvested herbs hanging from the rafters filled the air with comforting fragrances that reminded Addy of her Grandma's cooking.

"I'll be checking out the patterns on the feed bags, Jess. Get Grandpa's list of supplies, and I'll meet you at the counter to pay for the items."

"Will do." Jess pulled the list from his breast pocket and glanced at the shelves loaded with canned goods, and the barrels of nuts, crackers, and cucumber pickles. He made his way past the penny-candy tubs to the jars of honey.

Several women already stood by the stack of feed sacks, choosing their cloth for the next sewing project. The sage-green geometrics were popular, as were the red, white, and blue plaids. The newer flower patterns incorporated purple, pink, red, blue, yellow, and orange. Any color. Many designs.

Addy sighed. This was going to take longer than she imagined. She hoped Jess was a patient person.

As she bent over the muslin sacks, she overheard the conversations around her.

"Too bad the McIntyres are moving. The bank foreclosed on their house after the mister lost his job on the railroad."

"He spent his nights in the pub. His family went without. Now they are moving in with relatives in Missouri."

Other voices spoke. "Auction out at the Goodwill homestead next. Foreclosure on the property. William and his wife struggled hard to keep the land. They just needed a little more time."

"William was told to get his irrigation ditches in long before he dug them. With their access to the Big Thompson River, they should have been able to make it. Too bad. Three young'uns to feed and clothe."

"The bank should work harder to keep people on the land. There is no mercy with those financiers."

Addy tried not to tune into any more stray chitchat. The news unsettled her stomach.

As she fingered a bag of yellow, sunflower-designed fabric, the bullhorn quality of a man's speech caught her attention. Mr. Harry

Hamilton, the bank president. She crouched low so he wouldn't see her. This was the last parent she wanted to confront. But then, his words stiffened her spine.

"Yeah, Fred. I've gotten most of the land along the Big Thompson drainage system. That is worth more than gold. Those hick ranchers and farmers don't know what they're sitting on with water nearby."

"And they owe so little in taxes, Harry. If they got together, they could have bailed one another out, and then you would be sitting with cash, not land and water rights."

"Several homesteads got irrigation ditches dug by that Dettmann fellow. Their crops are just about ready for harvest. It would be too bad if the beets weren't sellable to the refinery."

"They say that farming is a gamble, Harry. Sometimes you win."

"And sometimes you lose." Harry and Fred finished the statement in unison with nasal-driven snarls.

"Well, gotta get a bag of flour for the missus," Hamilton concluded.

Addy peeked over her shoulder as Harry Hamilton hoisted a sack of flour and strode off between two packed aisles of supplies, his friend close behind his heels. She held her breath for a moment, trying to process what she heard. The stuffiness of the corner where she knelt closed in on her. With caution, she exhaled between pressed lips.

She chose four bags of chicken feed with cheery sunflowers woven into the fabric. She located Jess and a dolly and got the feed loaded onto the pick-up. In no time, she and Jess squeezed into the truck and drove to Hooverville with the apples.

She tried to keep her voice casual as she spoke. "Overheard a conversation while I picked out my fabric. That will teach me to mind my own business."

"Can't imagine it could be that bad." He switched to second gear as he glanced at her.

"Harry Hamilton and a companion named Fred talked about the foreclosures on the farms and ranches around here as gold mines because of their water rights. I had the distinct impression that some of the auctions were the result of manipulations by the bank."

"You're right in thinking that. Water is the only thing that keeps a homestead going, so only the ones who can connect with a water source will make it. These settlers bought the land cheap, so they don't realize how much it is worth. Most just want to call it quits and move on. The drought has taken the fight out of so many families who just can't hang on."

"Hamilton mentioned your name, and not in a good way. Your digging of irrigation systems has foiled his plans, I think."

"Addy, I need to share some of my background. Harry Hamilton and I have had many interchanges and most have been confrontational. He was on the elder council at the church where I was pastor before he took the job as bank president here. He opposed me when I tried to enforce the agreement between orphan riders and the deacons who fostered them.

"Those young people worked hard for their foster families because they had been promised a second chance at life, and then they were being denied their due. A person's word should mean something. Especially church men. Yes, I know Harry Hamilton and his sort of ethics." The wheels of the truck spun out dust clouds.

Jess pulled into his space by the trees and boulders. Before his boots hit the gritty ground, a man's deep voice broke the silence.

"Hey, Preacher. Didn't expect you on a Saturday."

Addy shot an inquisitive glance in Jess' direction, but he didn't react.

"Went to Yakima with a family needing some relief from dust pneumonia. That photographer, Arthur, pulled some strings and got them into a resettlement camp so the father can pick fruit for their board and room. The little girl's lungs were filling up, and, well, we both have experienced what comes next."

"Glad you were able to help. See you got some apples with you." The man thumped the side of the pick-up with his fist. "Look pretty tasty."

"They are all yours for the Hooverville folks. Just need one bushel so this young lady can put up a few quarts of applesauce." Jess indicated Addy with a nod of his head. "Addy, this is Calvin. He is the contact person for this group of displaced persons." Addy and Calvin shook hands. "Calvin, this is Addy who teaches at the school that Grandpa George's kids attend. She also has Harry Hamilton's son in her classroom."

Calvin's eyes darkened. "That's a young'un who needs to understand the meaning of work. I won't say no more. You have your hands full, Miss Addy. Come. Let me introduce you to someone who can show you around the shantyville while the preacher and I distribute the apples."

Nothing could have prepared Addy for the culture shock she experienced as they rounded the boulders. A small city emerged on the barren soil, a collection of large, box-shaped dwellings with doors and sometimes windows. Every imaginable scrap of wood, orange crate, cardboard, or fence post had been utilized to create these shelters from the sun, animals, or lack of privacy. A door might be a blanket, rows of spools strung on rope, or a wooden piece on hinges. Cooking pots on campfires dotted the walkway. As residents stewed and boiled their meals, the odors of cabbage and fish blended in the air. The cry of a baby startled her.

How could anyone raise a child in this environment? Where did the older ones go to school? How did they keep the disease rate down? Addy's observations rapid-fired questions into her brain.

"Grace. Come on over. I want you to meet someone." Calvin waved at a thin woman whose feed-sack dress drooped from her gaunt figure. She French braided her hair.

Grace padded barefoot on the dirt. "Hi, I'm Grace. Calvin's wife. I play the violin for the Sunday services, but I'm sure that the preacher told you about that." She winked at Jess.

"No, he didn't, but I suspect he will." Addy enjoyed the rise of red on Jess's cheeks. "I'm Addy, and I live with my Grandpa Meyers over near the Big Thompson River. We're here delivering some apples that Jess picked in Yakima. I want to put some up in jars this afternoon."

The men waved at the women and headed back to the truck.

"At the community building? I went there last year when I had something to can. Been a bit lean as far as food this year, but we hope to leave before the cold weather starts. Most of us are going to California, no matter what the border signs say about not needing more people." A tiredness that started deep inside Grace resounded in her words. "We just need enough money for gas for the cars."

Addy and Grace strolled between cooking pots, overturned orange crate chairs, and toddlers stacking pieces of wood into towers. Some girls dug a hop scotch into the dirt, and jumped from one square to another. Boys threw a ball made from tightly wrapped twine as they shouted to one another like the ball players on the radio. Kids displayed resilience. They created some fun with very little resources. Addy wondered how to make their lives better.

"Why is this place called Hooverville?" Addy gazed at a toddler dangling a piece of string for a cat to catch.

"When Herbert Hoover was president, many of his policies led to the collapse of banks, farms, construction, and businesses. This community is the result of a lot of bad decisions from his administration, so the name fits. There are Hoovervilles like this all over the country."

"But, where do the children go to school?"

Grace chuckled. "Well, now, that's an interesting question. Seems that squatters like us don't pay taxes so our kids can't go to any school around here. Many of the people who live in these shanties have an eighth grade education and work with the children in the afternoons so they know their sums, spell, and read. We share any books that we brought along, so a wide range of information is given. Those of us with musical instruments are teaching the next generation how to make music. Singing and playing an instrument can take the bad days and make them hopeful."

Addy kept close to Grace as she smiled at the tired, skinny women in their feed-sack dresses who slumped near their shanties. Many embraced toddlers, or showed signs of holding new life. The vacant-despair in some of the women's eyes alarmed Addy. Several times, her mother wore that look, and it scared Addy as a child. It scared her even more as an adult.

At one shanty, a young woman sewed pieces of cloth a mite larger than a postage stamp into rows. She had a stack of these odds and ends from feed sacks. She used a sense of pattern and color in her arrangement of these random scraps. The quilt she created with tiny stitches would be eye pleasing. Even in squalor, the spirit cried out for beauty. A lump rose in Addy's throat.

"You Jess's girl?" The woman's eyes glistened with mirth. "It's 'bout time that man settled down and got hitched."

Addy giggled. "Oh, no. We just brought some fruit to share with everyone."

"Well, if you say so. But y'all need to give that one a second look. Lots of gals here have done that already, and you're the only one he picked up on. I thank ya kindly for the apples. Can I give you some fabric for a wedding quilt as a gift?" The quilt maker handed Addy two scraps of feed sack, a solid navy blue piece and another one with thin light blue and white stripes.

Grace nodded at Addy, and she accepted the fabric.

"I'm grateful for the material. It will go well with the comforter I'm making. Hope you get yours finished soon. It looks like a cold winter." Addy shifted from one foot to another.

"We's goin' to California with the rest of this group. Only need a light quilt there. Be good to Jess. He deserves some happiness." Picking up her threaded needle, the woman chained on another little square. Addy folded the feed-sack scraps and put them in her pocket.

Jess's voice floated over a box-shaped wooden building. "That's the last of them, Calvin. I hope those apples make a difference."

"We've been needin' fresh fruit for a long time. Eatin' this will keep some of the diseases at bay."

"So, there is where you are." Grace addressed the men. "Got the apples distributed?"

"We were able to give every family three apples per person. It is only a start, but maybe some other fruit will become available soon." Jess's contented expression cheered Addy. "We'd love to stay, but Addy wants to can that last bushel of apples."

"So happy to meet you, Grace and Calvin. Hope we are able to connect again before you go to California." Addy shook Calvin's hand, but she hugged Grace like a sister.

Grace was like Grandma. They both faced the hardships of life with a belief that God would carry them through. *I'd give anything to be like that.*

As they headed for the pick-up, Jess's fingers circled Addy's tiny hand. She closed the gap between them, pressing her shoulder against his taut biceps, and let her heart beat like a tom-tom. But a lingering thought clouded the moment.

Would he turn out to be like all the men her mother knew?

Chapter 11

The building that housed the community canning facilities of the Ball Canning Company lay low on the city's profile. One story stucco with a flat roof and large windows that the Ball employees washed every day in the hopes of keeping a sanitary canning kitchen. The streaks on the glass testified to their efforts.

Addy carried the box containing pale blue Ball canning jars, rubber jar rings, wire bail glass lids, sugar, cinnamon, and a lemon from the general store. Jess lugged in twenty-one pounds of apples need for seven quarts of applesauce.

"My grandma used to can her vegetables and fruits here, even though she had all the equipment at home. I came with her one time when I was visiting in the summer." She set out her materials near the sinks of water.

"Why did she do that? Wouldn't it be easier to put up preserves at home?" He placed the apples on the tile floor.

"Oh, she did some small batches of jam and such in her own kitchen. But the bushels of produce were brought right here. She said it was a chance to talk to the women in the town. If people work together, they grow closer in their spirits, according to Grandma." Addy put the empty box to the side. "It was also an opportunity to use the latest canning equipment, get some new recipes, and have the preserves processed at a higher temperature than she could get at the homestead. Made sense to her."

Addy approached a woman standing near a stove. On her blouse, the word BALL was embroidered in blue letters.

"How much to water bath seven quarts of applesauce?"

"Three cents a quart if you use all your own materials. My name is Eva." The representative for the Ball canning jar company glanced at Addy. Her gaze lingered on Jess. "Been married long?"

Gulping, Addy stuttered. "We're just here to can some applesauce for my grandpa." She refused to even look at Jess.

"Oh," Eva leaned close to Jess. "Do you have any questions about this process? I can answer anything you want to know."

Addy dashed to the water basin. "Here, Jess. We can start by washing the dust off the apples. Come on over, and let's get the water going." She worked the pump handle to fill the basin.

Tapping Jess's shoulder, Eva spoke with a measured cadence. "Now, you be sure to come over to me if there is a problem." The Ball lady pulled her tomato-red lips into a toothy grin. With a swing of her hips, Eva sashayed across the room to aid a woman who filled her jars with cut-up potatoes.

Jess's gaze followed her. The realization straightened Addy's spine. It took a moment to get her mind back into the process of making applesauce.

"Are all the employees of these places so helpful?" Jess dipped his hands into the water and started to wash off apples.

"I doubt it. Eva is the friendliest Ball canning expert ever. Let's just do most of this work by ourselves. I think she's busy with other people." She glanced around the room as canners in different stages of the process worked on preserving food for the winter.

"What else do we have to do?" He was up to his elbows in water.

"You wash the jars and lids. I'll start peeling and coring these apples." She sat on a bench at a table with a wooden knife holder. Taking out a paring knife, she sliced into the thin skin of an apple. The challenge that Grandma gave her was to peel all the way around with a thin skin totally intact. One piece. As she listened to him run hot water, she focused on wielding her knife around the circumference of the apple.

"How well can you take off the skin of an apple?"

"Well, I figure that I can keep up with the women folks. What do you have in mind?" He held up his blade in one hand, an apple in the other.

"Just a little friendly competition. Count up how many times you slide off a skin in one piece of peel."

"I've had practice with potatoes. Okay. Let the best man win." He slipped his knife just under the red coating.

She focused on her skills. "Oops. This one broke."

"Ah, this one counts." He placed his trophy to the side. Sitting beside her, he peeled apples like a champ. One peel per apple. The stack of curly skins covered a newspaper that she brought. She planned to feed the cores and peeling to the chickens as a treat. After a few more turns of the paring knife, she declared him the winner.

"I guess all that practice digging ditches with precision translates into apple peeling." His pile overflowed the newspaper. She felt the heat of his body as he sat next to her. She took her time wrapping up the chicken's evening treat.

"Next step." She sterilized the glass jars, lids, and rings. The Ball Canning Company posted signs over each work station, explaining which steps to perform at that location. It made the process easier and allowed her to think on her own without bothering Eva.

They soon filled the large kettle supplied by the community canning center with apple chunks.

"'Put one inch of water in the bottom, then cook until tender.' Those are Grandma's instructions." She referred to her handwritten recipe.

He put the water in the pot and carried it to the stove. Using a wooden spoon, she stirred the contents to keep the apple chunks from sticking to the bottom and burning. He stood nearby, scanning the movements of other persons who canned carrots, tomatoes, potatoes, and beets.

"I remember helping to harvest the vegetables from the garden when I was a child."

"Did you help with the canning part?"

"No, that was woman's work. Our family divided chores by gender."

"But you help out in the kitchen at the homestead."

"Your grandmother taught me that all work is honorable. And so it is." He took the spoon from her and stirred the pot of applesauce.

A thin lady brought a pot of greens to the stove and turned up the heat on them.

"June! How many times have I told you that you can't do that?" Eva marched across the room and planted herself in front of June. The representative of the Ball Canning Company pressed her hands on her hips "We preserve food in this building, not weeds."

June's face burned scarlet, but she stood between Eva and the stove. "I take care of my family. This is what we got to eat this winter. Don't you pay no mind to what I do."

Deathly silence hung in the large space. Nobody moved. All eyes focused on the drama escalating over a pot of greens.

Eva's face muscles tightened. She tilted her head back, gazing upon June. "It is my job to be sure that nutritional foods are preserved. Besides, you don't have the money to pay for them to be pressure sealed. How do I know that they are safe for your family to eat?"

"I know I owe you money from the last time. But we need to eat." June shed no tears. Addy realized that her soul dried up a long time ago with her hope.

Jess stepped over to the women. Addy held her breath. She knew what angry women were capable of doing. Did he?

"Is it possible for me to pay for the pressure sealing of these jars of food, Eva? I know you are a reasonable woman working for a fine company. Nobody wants any problems today, do they?"

Low whispers and gasps crossed the room like gravel blown on a country lane.

Eva stood with a ramrod-straight back. "Tell this man what you are canning, and then let him think about if he wants to invest in weeds. Go ahead, tell him. Tell the whole world what you are feeding your family."

June worried the edge of her feed-sack apron as she gazed at floor. "Russian thistles. These are Russian thistles." Her words only cleared the first row of listeners, so information spread like echoes across the room.

A woman from the back shouted. "Ain't that a fancy word for tumbleweeds?"

After a group moan, nobody spoke.

"It is. Russian thistle or tumbleweed, call it what you will." Jess crossed over the floor to give June a side hug. "I've eaten my share of it. When you pick the young tender leaves, it's edible." Stepping to June's pile of greens, he picked up a handful. "Do you use a sauce on it, or eat it steamed?"

"I make a sauce so the little ones can eat a bowl of it." June glanced at Jess and answered with tears.

"I suspect you need some help. Looks like you have a lot of leaves to boil and can. Are these lamb's quarters? Those are good tasting too. We better get right to the canning before Eva closes this place on us." He picked up a spoon and stirred the greens before moving to a table with several bags of foliage. The leaves from tumbleweeds and lamb's quarters.

Eva stomped to the station where several women unloaded their batches of pickled beets. "None of this would happen in New York City." The canners shook their heads and clucked their tongues.

Addy added cinnamon to her applesauce and heated it up. Jess mashed the cooked apples into a fine sauce, then filled the seven quart jars, affixing the rings and lids. She pushed a cart over to the boiling water canner where the jars needed twenty minutes to seal the lids. Eva set the timer.

By the time Addy unloaded the applesauce, Jess and June wheeled over fourteen quart jars stuffed with green leaves.

"Fifty-two cents." Eva held out the palm of her hand to June.

Jess handed five dimes and two pennies to Eva. The Ball canning representative placed the jars in two pressure cookers. She rolled her eyes before setting the timer for twenty minutes.

June smiled for the first time. "Thank you. Thank you for everything," She smoothed her feed-sack dress with moss green geometric designs. The white rick-rack on the bottom held a few stray tumbleweed leaves.

"Just glad that we could help you out today. Life is sometimes hard enough. We all need to feel the grace of God once in a while." Jess finished wiping stray greens from the table.

How did he do that? How did he know what to say to people? How did he get to be so compassionate? Her mother's acquaintances never showed these types of emotions.

Eva pointed to Addy. "You can pick up your applesauce tomorrow. I have a shelf with your name on it. We need to let the contents cool and make sure the rings seal. All part of our service. Hope your experience with the Ball Canning Company was beneficial."

"We will never forget this day." Jess crooked Addy's arm in his elbow and hastened their pace to the exit.

They collapsed with laughter on the bench seat of the pick-up.

She held her sides as the laughter subsided. "Have you really eaten tumbleweeds?"

"Sure have. When there isn't anything else, you do what you have to do in order to survive. Before I came to your grandpa's, I lived with some road construction crews who needed dragline work. We ate whatever we could, when we could. Young tender tumbleweed tastes good fried up in a pan with bacon grease or stirred into a soup. That's why I appreciate what I have now. There was a time when I took everything in life for granted. Wish the hands of time reversed themselves, but they don't. It is a lesson I won't forget soon."

Cocking her head, she stared at a man who ate weeds and was grateful. They didn't make men like that anymore.

"June must have it really tough if she is canning tumbleweeds."

He paused. "The people in the Panhandle, Texas and Oklahoma, show a resourcefulness that is amazing. They survive on almost nothing but their faith. I've met some of these people in Hooverville. Others come from the surrounding area but were foreclosed on. Hooverville is the only place they can go to find shelter and community. Hopefully, this depression won't last much longer."

"Tell me a little more about the people in there." She slid over as far as she could on the seat of the pick-up. The stick shift prevented her from sitting any closer to him. She didn't want him to stop talking. The sound of his voice was so soothing. She wanted to nestle in his words.

"Well, you met Calvin and Grace. Both are musicians at the Sunday services where I preach. Calvin leads singing. Grace played violin in an orchestra before they lost their house in Omaha. Calvin's job in construction fell through as the economic base in Nebraska collapsed."

"That's awful. The same thing happened to so many people in Kansas too. Did they have a family to support?"

"Fortunately, their children are grown up and out on their own. Calvin and Grace didn't owe that much money on their mortgage, but the bank wouldn't extend their loan."

She gulped as she thought of Grandpa.

"Grace and Calvin were on their way to California, but ended up here when their money ran out. All these folks in Hooverville need just a bit of cash for gas. Then they can make it to work the harvest in the groves and truck farms. Wish there was a way to help them get that kind of money."

"You know what Grandma Martha would say, don't you?"

"'God will supply. Your job is to pray.'" They quoted Grandma in unison.

Jess slid his arm around Addy's shoulders as the empty truck bounced over potholes on the way to the homestead. Addy's heart said "yes" to the closeness of this man. But her head cautioned her to think before acting.

# # #

Driving with one arm around a desirable woman and one hand on the steering wheel of a trusty pick-up, Jess wanted to keep the wheels turning forever in the direction of the mountains. Get a cabin on a slope. Raise a garden and some children. Escape from all this dust. Could it happen?

He sighed as the lane circled into the homestead. Grandpa George sat on the porch waiting for them to park by the windmill. To Jess, that meant one thing.

Trouble must be brewing.

He squeezed Addy's shoulder, then opened the truck door. Grandpa strode toward them, his steps long for an older man.

"We need to talk, Jess. Let's see how that beet crop is coming."

Waving to Addy, he matched Grandpa George's pace as they headed for the acreage that promised to pay the bank two thousand dollars. From what he saw, he knew that the sugar beets would cover that amount with more left over. As far as the eye could see, rows and rows of perfectly formed beet tops formed green lines of potential cash.

Why was Grandpa George so anxious?

Chapter 12

Jess and Grandpa George navigated the fields until all they viewed beyond the well-irrigated rows of green and red beet leaves was a horizon of dusty, gritty earth. Tumbleweeds rolled in the gusts of winds that blew like ocean tides across the plains. The contrast between the well maintained farm and the drought ridden earth proved thc point that Hamilton made about water rights. The only way anyone could keep a grubstake was tied to a source of water.

"See all this." Grandpa George gestured over the beet crop. "This is what is standing between me or the bank owning this land." He reached in his back pocket. "Hamilton sent this. Got it today."

He unfolded a sheet of paper and read. "'Due to circumstances beyond our control, the date of your payment has been changed'. The bank moved it up a week. Why, these beets may not be ready by then. How can we harvest all this and get it to the sugar refinery that fast?"

Jess gazed out over acres of sugar beets, right on the cusp of harvest. Several rows of beet showed their shoulders out of the ground, ready to be picked. But it was too much work for Billy, Grandpa George, and himself. Even if Addy and RiverLyn helped, it would be a monumental job to get all the beets to the refinery in time. When he and Grandpa George planted the beets, they expected the harvest to be slow, methodical, and extend over a period of days. The weather needed to be less than seventy degrees but above freezing for the harvest. The window of opportunity proved thin.

Slamming his fist into his palm, Jess fumed. Hamilton must stay awake at night to think through all these details. His greed fueled this action. It just wasn't fair that he can got away with this.

"Here's the plan. One more good watering of the beets and a few more days of growth is all that they need to be ready to go. It will be close, and most beets will just make the minimum requirements of the refinery, but we can make it work. Hamilton won't get his hands on this homestead as long as we can work this field."

"Glad to hear this, Jess. I've been anxious all day. Haven't told the kids or Addy. Don't want to worry 'em with this. I know that Addy is being paid in script and that's Hamilton's doing. This is the first time the school has paid any teacher in that way. Figure it's Hamilton's way of making sure that we have no cash on hand." Grandpa George shook his head. "How does a man get to be so mean?"

That was a question which plagued Jess's mind for a long time. He just needed to be sure that the meanness did not overtake him too.

"Let's get a good night's sleep. Everything is always more manageable in the morning. I won't remind you of what Grandma Martha would say."

"Always wished that I had Martha's faith, Jess. Just wished that I had her faith."

# # #

Laughter peppered the air as Jess, Grandpa, RiverLyn, and Billy played Monopoly on a card table in the living room. The acquisition of houses, and now hotels, beefed up the competition among them. But the joke telling staved off any hostile feelings over the high rent exacted from Billy's four railroads. Fierce, but friendly.

Addy set out to make a quilt square for Katrina. The child's battle with dust pneumonia bothered Addy. Seeing children suffer from natural causes robbed her of sleep at night. Why did God let toddlers and youngsters get sick and die? Trusting Him like Grandpa and Grandma was not something she allowed herself the luxury of doing. Too many disappointments in life. Just one more crisis threatened to unravel her emotions like loose fibers on a burlap bag.

Making a quilt square in honor of Katrina soothed her concerns. Taking one scrap after another out of the fabric stash, Addy decided on a very delicate pink for Sunbonnet Sue's skirt, and pink flowers on a white background for the apron. A white bonnet with a piece of dark pink grosgrain ribbon for a hat band completed the outfit. Taking out Grandma's embroidery set, Addy created an apple with red thread which she placed in Sunbonnet Sue's hand. The apple in the square reminded her of Katrina's family as well as the woman who canned weeds for the winter. Both examples of the suffering so many people endured in these hard times.

Cutting with care, Addy created a Sunbonnet Sue appliqué from red and white material. She stitched it to white muslin. Digging into the stash, she found a small rectangle of black cotton. Using white embroidery thread, she printed ABC on it. With an under stitch, she sewed the slate to the hand of the stylized teacher.

A feeling of satisfaction washed over her as she surveyed a representation not only of herself, but her dream of sharing books and learning with children of the plains. She knew that Grandma Martha would be proud of her decision.

A smile pulled at her lips as she folded the two new squares with the growing stack of Sunbonnet Sues and Overall Sams.

After she put away her sewing supplies, she slipped into the kitchen. She took out a large sauce pan, then poured peanut oil into the bottom, and waited for the oil to heat.

"Making popcorn?" Jess's voice sounded close to her ear. Her stomach fluttered. She didn't hear him come into the room.

"I love popcorn in the fall. Especially on a Sunday night. Did you have a good service in Hooverville?" She stared at the pan, afraid to turn her head, afraid he would hear her heart pounding in her chest. His breath warmed her cheeks.

She watched from the corner of her eye as he leaned toward the table and picked up the metal container full of popcorn kernels. He handed it to Addy then stepped away from the stove and the hot oil.

"Calvin and Grace have a wonderful way of bringing music to the soul with the songs they select. They still haven't raised enough money to buy gas. They need to get started before the snow falls. Some are concerned about their children getting settled into a real school."

Addy poured the kernels into the saucepan and clamped a tight lid on top. She shook the pan over the heat. "Their problems are so helpless. Even Grandpa's difficulties are overwhelming. I try not to dwell on all of it and just do the best that I can each day."

"Oh, that's it. I'm done. No more money left." Grandpa stood up and left RiverLyn and Billy to finish. "How is that popcorn coming? I'm plumb out of everything in that game. But I outlasted you, Jess."

"That you did. I never did have a business head. Just know how to work."

Addy continued his thought. Jess gave things away. He was the type of man who would share his last meal or make sure another person was fed before eating himself. A good trait, but not one that made a man rich.

The lid covering the saucepan pushed on Addy's hand. She kept shaking until the sounds of popping kernels stopped. "Hand me that big bowl."

Jess took a ceramic bowl off the shelf and held it. She poured the white popcorn into the container, then reached for a small pan in the back of the stove. Melted butter dripped from the spout on the side onto the popcorn. Using a wooden spoon, she stirred it together.

"Are you just about done, kids?" Grandpa asked.

RiverLyn called from the living room. "We're puttin' the Monopoly game away. Billy won. He wiped me out of money in three rolls of the dice." In seconds, she and Billy joined the others at the kitchen table, scooping popcorn into cereal bowls.

"Speaking of being wiped out." Grandpa spoke with a full mouth. "How does it look for harvesting?"

"Checked the fields this afternoon. I think we need to soak them on Thursday, then start the harvesting on Saturday." Jess winked at Addy as she handed him a bowl of popcorn. "We'll foil Hamilton's plans and get this homestead paid off."

"Did I hear you talking about that greedy bank president? And school board leader?" Addy snapped her words as her voice raised to a high pitch.

"One and the same. You might as well know what's happening." Grandpa chewed on his snack. "Hamilton changed the due date for the two thousand dollars. It's pushed up a week."

"Can he do that?" Billy used a tone of voice reserved for playground bullies.

"Yeah, can he?" Addy wanted reassurances. What were they going to do?

"Sure can. He makes his own rules and gets away with it." Jess set his jaw. "The contract gives him a leeway for the harvest. He sets the due date, and that's that. Men like Hamilton use lawyers who know how to write up contracts so he can manipulate them. Grandpa either complies or loses this homestead."

RiverLyn whined. "But it's not fair. Isn't life supposed to be fair?"

"That's a whole discussion that I am not going to get into." Grandpa shook his head. "But I won't go down without a fight. Will you go to the bank with me tomorrow, Jess? Maybe Hamilton needs a dose of resistance."

"For all the good it will do, let's go. On behalf of all the other farmers and ranchers that he wants to defraud, let's go." Jess thumped the table with his fist.

"Finish up that popcorn, kids. We need to get to bed so we can face another week of school." Addy sat beside Jess and popped a kernel in her mouth. "Thank you for fighting for Grandpa," she whispered in Jess's ear as she snuggled close to his muscular shoulders.

She never remembered feeling as safe as she did in that moment.

# # #

As he laid out his custom sewn suit, tie, and shirt, Jess realized that he felt as home in his faded workday denims as he did in dress-up wear. Work boots or spit shined leather shoes. It didn't matter. His world vacillated between the hard-working, homeless, and well-to-do. He learned to be comfortable with all of them and to navigate in their cultural quirks. His time as a pastor taught him to respect honest men from every station of life. Knotting his silk tie, he relaxed in his clothes.

The Rocky Mountain Savings and Loan Bank occupied the whole corner of Main Street and First Avenue. A massive imposing structure built from custom brick and imported marble, the bank stood out from among the other businesses in their wooden or low-lying, common brick structures. The red stucco roof gleamed brightly in the morning sun. A testament to the control of the Hamilton family in this area of Colorado. An intimidating fortress for the wealth held in the bank's safe.

It was all about power. Just like the board of deacons and elders. He'd faced this before.

With slow strides, Jess and Grandpa George navigated the three marble steps to the brass- rimmed, oak entrance doors. The coolness of the quiet space settled Jess's nerves. As they approached the receptionist, their steps echoed in the cavernous foyer. A young woman with permed hair and a fashionable cotton dress off the racks of a Denver department store smiled with ruby-red lips.

"May I help you, gentlemen?"

"We come to speak to Harry Hamilton." Grandpa George laid it out there in no uncertain terms.

"Hmm." The receptionist scanned her daily log. "There isn't a scheduling for this time."

"Good. Then we aren't interfering with someone else's appointment. Please tell President Hamilton that George Meyers and Jess Dettmann are here to speak with him." Jess grasped his hat.

As the woman examined him from his hair to his shoes, he experienced a rush of blood flowing through his veins.

"Wait a moment." She disappeared behind a wall. The men waited until she reappeared. The receptionist batted her eyes at Jess. "Follow me, please," she directed in a breathy voice.

They trailed her down a hall to two glass-paneled doors. She opened them and made her announcement. "This is George Meyers and Jess Dettmann to see you, sir." As they stepped into the room, she closed the doors behind them.

Harry Hamilton lounged on an overstuffed chair behind an imposing oak desk filled with papers, pens, ink, and framed photos. Jess recognized the picture of Hamilton's son, Harry Junior.

"Have a seat. Hope the beets are flourishing, Mr. Meyers. And Mr. Dettmann. How is that earth moving machine of yours doing? Dug any more spud cellars?" Hamilton examined his fingernails. "Now, what is so important that you are taking up my time?"

Pursing his lips, the bank president smoothed the sleeve on his silk-blend, custom-stitched jacket. Jess recognized the trademark styling as that of a reputable tailor who owned a shop in Omaha and apprenticed several orphan train teens.

Hamilton was pompous. Just like Jess expected.

"I want to talk about moving the date for the money that I owe. A week makes a lot of difference when it comes to harvesting beets, as you well know." Grandpa George leaned forward in his chair. He tugged at the knot of his frayed tie, and hunched his shoulders in a nappy suitcoat one size too big for his frame.

"Well, now, Mr. Meyers. The time to have squabbled about due dates was before you signed a contract. As you are aware, the tax money and other loans need to be paid so that our teachers here in the town high school and our one rural school teacher can be paid in cash, not script. My concern is for the educators and the responsibility of the school board to them." Hamilton steepled his fingers and smirked.

Angry thoughts shot through Jess's mind. Fake piety. He didn't care about the teachers. Hamilton's heart was greedy. All he wanted was to own every homestead that had access to water. Especially Grandpa George's spread.

Grandpa George squirmed. "If you go back to the original date, then I'll be able to pay. Otherwise, it may be difficult."

"I'm sorry, Mr. Meyers." Hamilton dragged out the words. "If I make concessions for you, then who knows where that will lead with the rest of the ranchers and farmers around here. They are a pessimistic group who will want to take advantage of me."

"Pessimistic?" Jess heard the calm strength in his voice. "A Colorado homesteader is the most optimistic person alive. A farmer will keep looking for a gray, rain-filled cloud coming over the mountains even if it has been years since precipitation fell. A rancher living on the plains roams the countryside with his herds finding places for them to graze, filled with optimism that a grassy slope is behind the next hill."

Gesturing toward Grandpa George, Jess continued. "Mr. Meyers has the most positive attitude of anyone I've ever known. He already has plans to plant potatoes next year for a rotation on the soil. No, Mr. Hamilton, you can never accuse the men in this county of being pessimistic."

Jess stood.

Grandpa George shut his jaw-slacked mouth. "Thank you for listening, Mr. Hamilton. We will be back with your money on time."

"Been our pleasure to talk with you." Jess held out his hand, but Hamilton fussed with papers on his desk.

"Don't be late, Meyers. You know what has happened to others who didn't pay on time."

Jess took his words to be a threat. What did Hamilton have up his sleeve? If the son was anything like his father, no wonder Addy experienced problems at school.

Jess opened the glass-paneled doors, and they strode out of the bank in silence.

On the sidewalk, Jess led the way back to the pick-up. "I don't trust Hamilton. He has a trick or two to play, and I don't know what that might be. But, I do know that God will watch over us if we trust Him for guidance."

"That bank president strikes me like a low-down snake-in-the-grass, that's what. I've heard how he pushed others out of their land stakes. Been prayin' that the Good Lord will take care of me and the kids."

"Keep that optimistic spirit, Grandpa George. You know Martha would have one too. She talked to me once and said something I've always remembered. 'Don't pray to be sheltered from dangers, but to be fearless when facing them.'"

As the two drove back to the homestead, conviction flooded Jess. He stood up to the church board in Omaha, and after the victory, left. That mistake followed him to his present situation. No more running for him. No more caving in to the bullies. He would make his stand with Grandpa George and the homesteaders of Weld County against the abuses of the bank president.

Fearless. That's what he needed to be.

Chapter 13

As Addy, RiverLyn, and Billy approached the school building, the ravages of northwest winds grew more apparent. Being two miles farther from the mountains made a huge difference in the effects of weather. The pile of dirt on the entrance steps needed to go.

"I'll get the shovel out of the lean-to and start clearing off the doorway." Billy handed his lard pail to RiverLyn, then ran to the lean-to. Within moments, dirt flew all around him. Addy and RiverLyn scrambled by Billy's whirlwind cleaning and entered the classroom.

"Needs a dusting, Addy. I'll do that before I get the slates and chalk ready." RiverLyn hung up the lard pails on hooks, then grabbed a cloth rag from a small pile.

"Let's see. I have the lower grade's work on the board." Addy thought aloud. "Maybe some harder math problems for the eighth grade boys. Give them a challenge."

RiverLyn snickered. "Serves 'em right for not learnin' all these years. They got a lot to do to git ready for the grade school final exams."

"Well, thank goodness they are applying themselves at the beginning of the year. It wouldn't do them any good in the spring to try to catch up." Addy stepped back from the board to examine her work. "That will do just fine."

Billy burst through the door. "Done. What else can I do?" He closed the door after him.

"Just prepare to meet the day. We have a lot of material to cover in history."

A turn of the door knob and Lillian entered. "Good morning, Miss Meyers." She hung up her lard bucket and sat on the bench, opening up a book to read.

Addy realized how fortunate Lillian was to have so many cousins in Chicago who sent their used books to her. Most of the books hardly showed any wear at all. Her clothing also arrived twice a year in the same box as the literature, according to Lillian. That's why she wore some nicely made dresses and even shoes.

Several other students drifted in the door, then sat at their seats. Melvin and Claude meandered in and settled in the back, poking each other in the ribs.

The clock needed one more movement of the minute hand, and then Addy's day could start. She inhaled, ready to announce the pledge to the flag when clamoring feet outside the door caught the classroom's attention. Harry stomped into the room, hunched over. His father followed him.

"Miss Meyers, may I speak with you privately?" Mr. Hamilton did not ask a question. He issued an order. "Outside."

"Okay. Boys and girls, just start your seat work. You know what I expect." Addy exhaled through pressed lips, and shook her fingers in the folds of her skirt to relieve the tension that raced through her body.

Yesterday, Grandpa and Jess visited this man as the head of the bank. She needed to deal with him as her employer.

Not an ideal situation.

She left the door ajar so the students remained in her view as she stood next to Mr. Hamilton on the clean-swept steps to the school house. The muscles behind her knees strained.

"Yes, yes, yes." Hamilton intoned. "I can see that you are doing a fine job on the maintenance of the building both inside and out. These surprise visits allow me to keep my eye on how well our students are getting educated in this school. Which brings me to the purpose of my visit." Hamilton's brows deepened over his squinting eyes. He stood very straight, giving him a decided height advantage over her as he stared down on her.

Don't feel intimidated, Addy reminded herself. Remember how Jess and Grandpa kept their heads about them.

"Feel welcome to visit our classroom at any time, Mr. Hamilton. You will see learning taking place every day." She tried to keep her voice steady.

"Every day? Really? Is that true, Miss Meyers?" The school board president's voice seeped between clenched teeth. "From what the townsfolks say, there was an unsanctioned baseball game played here about a week or so ago. Took up over an hour of class time. Rumor has it that you ran the bases in your dress."

Her heart thumped like a rabbit's foot thumping on a log. "Yes, it is true. The students need a break from their academics every once in a while to keep them on their toes. Using recess and physical education to help focus learners is one of the new approaches I learned in teacher training."

"Hmm. Seems like a waste of time that should be spent drilling on math. Which is why I am here. Harry is my heir, and needs to become proficient in his numbers. From what he is doing on Saturday in the office, that boy is behind in just about every subject in school." Mr. Hamilton's index finger wagged in front of Addy's face like the tail of a puppy begging for treats. Protective instincts pulled her back.

"Don't think that I can't make your life miserable, Miss Meyers. For you and your grandpa and even that dragline preacher who is interfering with things he needs to leave alone. When and if your script gets paid is one hundred percent up to me. So, your job is to make my boy into an educated young man by the spring exams. Do it." As he spoke, spit from his words peppered Addy's cheeks.

She recoiled.

"Or else."

Mr. Hamilton marched toward his automobile. Then he turned back to Addy. "Go. Do your job, Miss Meyers, while you still have one." He folded his body behind the steering wheel and started the ignition. Pulling away, he left a trail of dust mixed with the car's exhaust.

Addy shivered in the warm October sun. She inhaled and exhaled several times before entering the classroom to start the morning routine. It wasn't fair that her pay was being held back. It wasn't fair that the bank picked off the homesteaders around the area.

She stared at the pupils seated in the classroom, their lives tenuous. Would the next sale be one of their homesteads? It wasn't fair that Hamilton intimidated her grandfather and all the hardworking ranchers. Even RiverLyn recognized that the bank wasn't fair when it moved up the payment dates.

She rose to her full height. She would do whatever it took to stand up to the injustice of it all. If she didn't fight for the homesteaders, then she would never be able to face herself. If she didn't fight for her job by making the eighth graders pass their graduation exams, then she deserved to lose this position.

She knew what to do and would give it everything within her.

She strode back to where the eighth grade boys hunched over their work.

"We have a lot of ground to cover, young men. Those eighth grade proficiency tests are hard. But I know you can do it." She leaned over the table, staring into the eyes of each of the young men with a steady gaze.

"Are you in? Or are you out?"

The Regulator clock on the wall ticked away the seconds as the other students quieted their shuffling so they could listen in on the conversation with the big boys. The odor of souring milk in canning bottles tinged the air.

"I'm in." Claude shook his red hair out of his face.

"Me, too. I'm in." Melvin encircled Claude's shoulders with his arm.

Addy and the two boys turned to Harry. He ground his teeth, then smirked.

"Oh, I am so in." The words slid from his lips in a long, slow, deliberate manner. He joined the group hug. "I'll show my old man that I'm not as stupid as he thinks."

"Good, then I need to get a strategic program in place for the three of you. It won't be easy for any of us, but it will be worth it when you take the exam in Greeley with the town kids and pass. Your parents appear to be optimistic, but you and I know that they don't realize how far behind you have become." Addy paused to be sure she held eye contact with each one of the three students. "This is just the type of challenge that will take everything we've got."

Addy turned toward the large black chalkboard. "Let's get started. Now, how do you attack the word problem on the board about the pounds of crops per acre?"

The afternoon sped by as fast as a fish swimming down the Big Thompson River.

After the students left, Billy swept the floor. He leaned on the broom. "Why're you givin' those boys a chance? They deserve to flunk eighth grade."

"Yeah. I was thinkin' what Billy just said." RiverLyn stopped dusting the chalk tray.

"Last week, when Claude was in the cloak room, he said he was gonna git you just like he did the last teacher. Git you fired. Do you really trust him?" Billy gripped the broom with tight fingers.

Addy pondered her answer. "Well, it isn't easy to not want revenge. I confess that it would vindicate me if they failed the final exams. But, then, what kind of teacher would that make me? Not one that any person should admire. No, I guess I thought about this during the last few days. It was Grandma who made the choice."

"How could Grandma do that?" RiverLyn asked.

"I just kept thinking about how she handled situations. She always made allowances for folks to mess up and then get a second shot at making amends. Those people did the right thing and were better off for it. Guess I believe that our three students got caught up in power struggles with teachers and didn't know how to back down. Now that the consequences of their actions are getting them in trouble, they need a little help to work their way back. I can do this. After all, I am an adult."

Billy put the broom into the closet. "Do you know who is gettin' sheriffed next?"

"I don't know what that means."

"Merle Murphy was talkin' about how the sheriff comes to a homestead and sells off everything. It happens real sudden. The kids just disappear from school. It happened a couple of times before you came."

"Merle is referring to a foreclosure. I hope it doesn't affect any child in this school."

Billy shut the closet door. "I wouldn't count on anything. Getting sheriffed is out of a kid's control."

Chapter 14

Addy strode to Jess's log cabin and knocked on the door. "Wake up, Jess. Wake up."

She hated to ask him for help, but what else could she do? She couldn't go to Grandpa and expect him to understand how she felt.

"Want to join me in feeding the chickens?" A deep voice from behind startled her. She turned to face Jess.

"You're up early for a Saturday morning." He held up an empty feed bucket. "I just took care of our fowl friends."

She spoke with rapid-fire words. "I want you to go with me to the Goodwill homestead auction. The sale concerned some of my students. They kept asking who will get sheriffed next? Their parents work so hard. How can a nation support a law that takes away a man's farm? His livelihood? His life?"

She paused as she willed her heart to stop breaking. The warmth of his body permeated her as he stood close to her. How she longed for him to put his arms around her and say that everything would be alright. "It will help me to understand what Grandpa is facing if Hamilton's bank forecloses on him too."

"Is that a good idea? Are you prepared to see the auctioneer sell someone's life work? Only to satisfy a bank loan that could be paid off if a reasonable plan was made? Can you handle the disappointment? Sometimes the family gets emotional. This can go ugly real fast. At some foreclosures, there has been violence." Jess's gaze pierced into her soul. "Are you ready for that?"

Her voice hitched. "Yes. I have to know what we're up against."

"Then, let's have a cup of coffee and a biscuit with Grandpa George. Best we not tell him where we are going. It might be upsetting to him."

"Okay. But we need to get going if we want to get to the Goodwill homestead by eight o'clock." Addy started for the house with Jess at her side.

Before the sun rose above the Rockies, Jess drove the pick-up in a cloud of tire-spun dust down the road to the other side of the Big Thompson River. The green foliage of potatoes or beets near irrigation ditches ran from the river onto the farms close to the source of mountain-fed water. The further away from the river, the drier the land and the higher the sand dunes. Only rough grass and tumble weeds grew from the ground where the dust storms stripped away the topsoil in massive, wind-driven clouds. The seriousness of the farmers' situation sobered Addy. She tried to be light hearted, but the further Jess drove, the more she understood the consequences from drought and dust on the land.

"Look at that line up of buggies and cars. Seems like the whole county turned out." Jess eased the pickup close to a fence.

"The sheriff's squad car is parked near the windmill."

"Guess they expect trouble. Realistic guess."

Three deputies circulated among the gathering hoard as the sheriff stood near the auctioneer. Men in suits mingled with cowboys in chaps and farmers in bib overalls. All wanted to know the worth of this homestead near the Big Thompson River, as it held water rights. Each person had a different reason for needing that information.

"I didn't know that there would be so many people here." She was glad she wore cowboy boots as she trudged in the sand. "Looks like there is a crop of potatoes that could be harvested soon. Couldn't that generate enough money to pay off the debt?"

He leaned in to answer. "Probably would cover their immediate loans. Get them through the winter. That's why the bank moved up the date. So the homesteader has no money and will default."

"Hear about the sales in the Dakotas?" a gentleman in a gray suit asked his companion. "The owner got really upset about the sale and fights broke out. Lot of people got hurt."

"Those auctions didn't have the law with them. Hamilton has made sure that there will be no trouble here. You can count on that." The other man pulled a silver pocket watch from his vest. "Got five minutes to go."

Jess stared straight ahead as if he hadn't listened to the conversation, but he tapped Addy's arm with his elbow to let her know that he heard.

Two women stood near her. Their chatter caught her attention.

The woman dressed in fabric from a blue feed bag shook her head. "The Goodwill homestead owes so little money. If everyone just waited until next year. If it rained, then a new crop would come in. Maybe things would be different."

"Next year. Next year. That's all my husband wants. I hate to say it, Martha, but there will never again be rain in these parts. The topsoil is gone and more dusters stack up the dirt. If a farmer isn't hitched to an irrigation ditch, there is no hope for any cash crop." The speaker puckered her lips.

Next year. If it rains. That was what everyone hoped for. It was the only thing left for the homesteaders. Addy swallowed the lump in her throat.

The chatter of fifty or more men toned down to muted voices. The people focused their gaze on a man with salt-and-pepper hair as he strutted into the yard. He examined the few pieces of equipment that were for sale. Two surly younger men trailed along with him. By the faded blue jeans and soft boots that they wore, Addy assumed that they were mutton punchers from the mountain area. With the air of a predator, the older man's stare fixed on one person and another in the crowd.

"It's the Murphys. Things will heat up." The speaker wore denim clothes with wool-lined footwear.

"Heard that they kept the price so low on the Asberry place that the bank made no money at all." The farmer in bib overalls picked his teeth with a straw.

The sheep rancher scratched behind his ear with a calloused finger. "Wonder what they're up to here. Can't be good."

Addy moved a little closer to Jess.

His arms hung loose at his side. "I've seen men like Patrick Murphy before. When you throw them to the wolves, they return leading the pack. Life doesn't get them down. I suspect he's here for a reason."

"His son, Merle, is in my class. Signs of poverty cover him, but he's wiry and a hardworking student." Addy hadn't met Merle's father, but spoke with the mother once.

The sheriff loped over to the trio. "Nice day for a sale, eh, Patrick?"

Addy and Jess leaned in to listen.

"Sure and it is." Patrick Murphy ran his chapped hand over the blades of a plow.

"How are the sheep getting along?" The sheriff directed his question at the young men.

"Been grazin' in the mountains. Will git a good flock goin' by spring." The taller lad with long, reddish hair answered.

Patrick Murphy tensed into a stance that reminded Addy of a cougar poised on a mountain rock.

The auctioneer stood up on a wooden box and raised his mallet. "It is a fine day to auction off a fine farm of thirteen hundred acres close to a water source. There is a good house and a strong barn with a windmill. When the rains return, this land will be prosperous."

The auctioneer omitted the fact that this day was tragic. A family was losing everything they worked for over the years for the lack of very few dollars. Just because the law was on the bank's side and the sale was legal did not make it right. Injustice roiled inside her like water boiling in a tea kettle.

"Let's have a bid. Anyone bid me one thousand dollars?"

The action started. A man from Nebraska bid fifteen hundred.

Then a suitcase farmer bid two thousand. Addy resented the city folk who bought up acreage, then paid poor farmers to do the work of bringing in a cash crop for them while they lived in luxury in an Eastern city.

The well-dressed man with the pocket watch shouted out, "Three thousand."

Silence.

Addy noticed a hawk soaring overhead. The bird of prey circled the homestead, scoping out its next victim.

This whole farm was worth more than that. Grandpa's debt was nearly that much. Why couldn't the potato crop be sold first and the rest of the money negotiated over time? Greed. It boiled down to greed from the bank. She refused to let this happen to Grandpa.

No one else bid.

"Three thousand." The auctioneer raised the gavel over his head. "That will be three thousand, once." He surveyed the crowd.

Patrick Murphy and his sons moved like rattlesnakes through the crowd toward the city slicker with the high bid. As the three Murphys surrounded the man with the money, a ruckus started over by the barn. Two boys pounded the wall of the barn with hard balls, creating a loud, banging noise in the anticipatory quiet. The sheriff and his deputies elbowed their way over to the two youngsters. The ball tossers ran away with the law in hot pursuit.

The auctioneer leaned into the crowd, focusing on the men in suits. "Three thousand twice."

When the law disappeared out of sight, Murphy grabbed the high bidder by the throat. Addy gasped. Jess leaned toward the two men, his body tense.

Murphy hissed. "You gave the winning bid?"

"Yes." The voice squeaked.

"If you don't withdraw that bid, you'll never make it to the train at dusk. Have you been listenin' to the coyotes at night? They sound mighty hungry to me."

The man paled.

"Last call. Three–"

"Auctioneer!" Murphy's voice cut through the air with clarity. "This man wants to reconsider his bid. Let my boys go help you out, sir." The young men approached the auctioneer with a swagger. The crowd melted in their path. "Now, are there any other bids for this property?" Murphy surveyed the prospective buyers, keeping his hand on the back of the gentleman's throat.

"I bid ten dollars." The words came from a woman.

Addy recognized the voice. Eva, the woman who ran the community canning center.

The auctioneer protested. "But you're the sister of the homesteader."

The crowd mumbled in angry tones as they stepped toward the lone auctioneer.

The bid stood.

"Ten dollars once, ten twice, ten three times. Sold." The gavel fell hard on the small table beside the auctioneer whose brow dripped with sweat on a fall day.

The crowd sighed. Within a few minutes, the sheriff and the two deputies rounded the side of the barn with the two boys in tow. In the hush that lay over the gathering, the sheriff asked if the homestead sold.

"It did. But for only ten dollars." The tight tone in the auctioneer's voice hinted at the coming wrath he would experience from Hamilton.

"Who is going to pay for the bank's fees, or for this auction?" The sheriff wailed as the smiles on the crowd grew broader with every remark from the officials.

Jess and Addy watched as Eva waved a ten-dollar bill while she hugged her brother and his family. Addy joined the women in the group as they all cried tears of relief and joy. Glancing around, she couldn't spot the Murphy trio. Somehow, they slithered back to their sheep ranch in the mountains without any fanfare.

She dabbed her cheeks with the handkerchief she always carried in her skirt pocket. Jess sauntered into the crowd, greeting a rancher, shaking hands with an investor, slapping the back of a cowboy in his path. He left people with smiles and a sparkle in their eye. She couldn't hear what he said, but whatever it was, it brought encouragement to the person he met. Most of the crowd had dissipated when he moseyed back to her.

"Sorry to keep you waiting." His voice was husky. "I like to get to know the people of the area. So many needs. So much pain behind those smiles. A good word heals like medicine."

"No problem. It gives me an opportunity to watch the law at work." She tipped her head in the direction of the auctioneer and the sheriff. They sat hunched on a log. The deputies mixed with the last groups of men to head off for their homes.

Jess sighed. "I am not a betting man, but I would lay money on the fact that Eva signs the homestead back to her brother. This auction sends a message to Hamilton that the bank can't just keep buying up the farms for pennies on the dollar. It means that he will step up his techniques for future foreclosures. I do believe that Grandpa George is next on the docket." Worry lines creased his brow.

Who will step in with just the right amount of money to satisfy the bank? The Goodwill homestead was able to outsmart Hamilton and his associates, but the banker would be up to new tricks when it came time for Grandpa. How could they anticipate their moves? It was up to her to raise the money. But how?

"Better be gittin' along." One of the deputies called out to lingering groups. "Another duster is due south of here. Ya' don't wanna git caught in it."

Jess and Addy joined the caravan leaving the homestead. They drove single file down the one vehicle lane for several miles. Away from the Big Thompson River and the irrigation ditches that provided water for potatoes or sugar beets. A few cows fed on straggly grass amid the tumble weeds. A rattlesnake side-wound down a sand dune, then blended in with the gritty soil. How could any living creature survive in the dust and dryness?

"You just saw some of my work, Addy. The Goodwill homestead was one of the first places I dug irrigation ditches. It helped those folks get some cash crops to offset the beef that they sold to stay in good with the bank. Would have broken my heart to see them lose their land. They worked so hard and have so little. Just doesn't seem right that Hamilton's greed can rob God-fearing families out of the meager belongings they have. The law needs to be rewritten to protect the working class."

"Have you dug any other ditches around here?"

"Probably most of them. There aren't too many men who want to do the kind of work that I do. But, it is fulfilling to help out newlyweds or old timers who work with nature to make a living in a hard time. Right here in Weld County, we don't bear the brunt of the Dust Bowl the way those in Oklahoma and Texas do. Some can get by with sheep or cattle, and those near a river can raise a crop that will keep body and soul together. We have a lot of blessings that other folks don't have."

All Grandpa George wanted in life was to live on his plot of land and eke out a living. It seemed so reasonable. How could she make sure that he could live out his days on the land he loved? She worried the seam of her dress.

"I hope the Murphys don't show up at another auction."

"Why?" She hoped that they attended every one.

"Their strong-arm tactics can be effective only once. Bullying people is not the answer to the bank's greed. This route only leads to violence in the end. We must make sure that Grandpa George does not face this type of situation."

"How?"

"I don't know for sure, but I am certain that our help comes from the Lord. He knows how to work all this out in a civil manner."

Your faith is stronger than mine, Jess. But I want mine to grow.

The windmill, chicken coop, barn, and house finally loomed into sight. RiverLyn and Billy ran down the lane to greet them like tumbleweeds rolling in a gale. He slowed the pick-up, then stopped. The two children climbed in. Addy's arm brushed Jess' bicep. Her heart raced from the skin on skin tingle.

"Did they sell the ranch? How much? Did they get in a fight with the sheriff?" The children fed one question after another faster than a chicken pecking at corn kernels.

"We'll tell you all about it when we talk with Grandpa. By the way, who is that with him?"

RiverLyn spoke up. "Oh, that's Albert. He's a hobo. Grandpa invited him to lunch with us."

"Hmm. Is that a good idea?" Addy recalled hobos in Topeka. Her mother found a piece of bread to make a sandwich or an egg to fry for these shabby men. Their neediness scared Addy, so she stayed in the house while her mother fed them on the porch.

"These men are displaced." Jess surveyed the man. "Some good. Some with problems that can't be solved. But we need to show hospitality. Grandma always had something for them to eat."

"We been doin' this for a long time, Addy. We're far out so we don't git too many hobos." Billy hung his elbow out the open pick-up window just like Jess.

The four joined Albert and Grandpa on the porch. A faint odor of unwashed body and clothes wafted from Albert. Several weeks of whiskers sprouted from his cheeks. His shoes held together even with laces. Sandy brown hair hung limp and scraggly around his neck. A piece of rope tied his too-large trousers onto his lean frame. Addy didn't know where to start helping him get back to civilization.

"I need to make lunch, Grandpa. Maybe you could show Albert where the wash tub is. Billy, bring some hot water for him." She motioned to the barn.

"Be pleased to wash up, miss. It's been a long time since I've had a place to do that." The flush on his cheeks told her all she needed to know.

She smiled, then set to boiling lots of hot water for Jess and Billy to take to the barn. Once she put on a pot of pork and beans she cooked the day before, she sliced corn meal mush to fry in a skillet with bacon grease.

"RiverLyn, set the table. Pour some milk into glasses, while I put on a fresh pot of coffee." Grandpa would want her to use the coffee, even if it cost a lot of money. He and Grandma always gave their company the best that they had. This was the best. Grandma would be proud of her.

Addy stirred the beans and listened to the clinking of dishes behind her. The aroma of freshly brewed coffee and fried mush made her realize how hungry she was after a long morning. She turned around with a platter of fried mush cakes as the door opened. Catching her breath, she tried not to drop the plate.

"Albert. Is that you?"

The man standing in the kitchen, followed by Grandpa, Jess, and Billy, did not resemble the hobo who sauntered into the barn to wash up.

"Why, Mr. Albert. You look good." RiverLyn nodded her head.

Albert's shaved cheeks reddened. "I am obliged to all of you for makin' me feel so much at home. Jess here gave me these duds to wear, as well as the shoes. Your grandpa cut my hair so it don't hang down so much. And now I git to eat with a family. It's almost more than a man can take in at one time." His voice hitched.

As the group seated itself at the table, Addy again glimpsed the depths of deprivation from the Dust Bowl.

Grandpa bowed his head. "Bless this food, and bless Albert as he goes on his way to find a job. Give him the hope that can only come from a resting on You. Amen."

Everyone echoed the amen.

"Tell us about yourself, Albert." Jess scooped some beans from the pot in the middle of the table and put it in Alberts's bowl before he served himself.

"Well, I was a clerk at the country store in Dove's Corner, Texas, until all the dusters started moving the dirt around." Albert stopped to take a bite of the corn mush. "This is mighty good food, miss. Anyway, the farmers and ranchers got their supplies on credit at the store. After a few years, nobody could pay back their tabs, so my employer went out of business. I kept the books, too, because I learned my math in school. He lost a lot of money. Most of the town folk just got up and moved away to live with relatives in other states."

RiverLyn leaned in. "Is that what you are doing, Albert? Going to stay with relatives?"

"Wish I had someone to go live with, but there just isn't anyone who needs another mouth to feed. My parents died of dust pneumonia. My brothers have their hands full with little ones. I hear tell of a Civilian Conservation Corps just north of here that is run by Hugh Bennett. The government needs help planting trees and bulldozing dunes. I 'spect that I could do that."

"I heard in town that Bennett wants to plant trees to make a windbreak. He thinks that it will keep the dusters from being so fierce and taking more topsoil off our land." Jess poured coffee for Grandpa, Albert, and himself. "If Bennett and the government have their way, there will be trees growing from Texas to the Canada border. They call the group the CCC for short. Hope you can qualify for the work."

"How long you been on the road?" Addy asked.

"About three weeks. Stopped in a Hooverville and stayed one night there. Just been walking, making my way to Bennett's headquarters so I can sign up. It don't pay so much that I will get rich or anything, but it is a 'hot, cot, and a pot', if you don't mind me saying so."

Jess sipped coffee from his mug. "How many men are on the move?"

"Thousands. Most ride the rails trying to git to a place where there is work. California put up signs that they don't want nobody who isn't already working. I tried getting on a train car, but figured it was too dangerous for me. So I'm walkin'." Albert smiled as Jess scooped up more pork and beans for him. He sopped up the juice with a bit of corn meal mush.

When the meal ended, Grandpa pulled out a lard pail. "Pack that feller a bite to eat, Addy. He still has a ways to go to git to where that Bennett runs a work camp."

Addy made sandwiches with a bit of honey and butter. She filled a Mason jar with water.

"I'm going to drive Albert as far as the South Platte River. I think he can get a ride on a boat or barge there. Someone will know how he can connect with the CCC." Jess grabbed his straw hat off the hook on the wall. He handed it to Albert. "You'll need this if you work in the sun. Take it with our blessing."

Addy knew that Jess did not have another hat for his own work in the sun, but she kept silent.

Albert adjusted the hat on his head, then twisted his hands together before speaking. "Y'all remind me of the church folk when I was young like Billy. My ma and pa took me to meetin's then. Haven't gone back since they died. Now, I think I'll try to find a church somewhere. It's time to reconnect with what I was taught. Life has been hard for me, but maybe I can make it better. Thank y'all for the kindness." He took the Mason jar and lard bucket from Addy and held them close to his body.

RiverLyn, Billy, Grandpa, and Addy waved to the green Ford pick-up long after it blended in with the sandy lane. They wanted Albert to know how much they cared.

That could be them next, if Hamilton had his way. A shudder pearled down Addy's spine. There had to be a way to beat the bank. But how?

Chapter 15

Grandpa and Jess stood near the gate to the irrigation ditch. Addy and the children left for school already, the chores were done, and the task of harvesting many acres of the beet crop loomed ahead. There were a lot of preparations before that could happen. A lot.

"Looks like the beets grew to a good size for making sugar." Grandpa shaded his eyes against the rising sun as he surveyed the fields. "Just like the Great Western Sugar Company wants them. The shoulders of the beets are protruding from the soil." He leaned to push aside some dark green foliage. "The deep red and smooth skin show real quality. Yep. They're ready." The weight of the task before Grandpa sobered him.

"This harvest should bring in some cash. I hope it's enough to get the bank off your back and leave you some money for spring seeding.

Next year, it just may rain, and we won't need to count on melted snow and irrigation as much as we have this season." Jess reached down and fingered the dry dirt. "We'll flood the fields a day or two before picking the beets to loosen them up. When do you want to do that?"

"How about tomorrow? Give them all one more day to grow into their prime. It appears that we have just about made it to the finish line. Always makes me wonder when the next shoe will fall. Hate to be a pessimist, but the last few years have not made me believe that things will go without a hitch."

Jess put his hand on Grandpa George's shoulder. "I've prayed over these fields as we sowed the seed. I've been praying over them as the seedlings grew. One more time, I will pray. God, give us a harvest that will be a blessing to this family. Amen."

Gravel crunched under a car's tires. Jess and Grandpa George to turn toward the lane. The sheriff's black sedan kicked up a cloud of dust behind it as the vehicle sped into the parking area by the windmill. The uniformed man stepped onto the gritty barn yard. He adjusted his holster before taking long strides in their direction.

This couldn't be good news for Grandpa George from the look on that man's face. *Lord, keep my tongue civil and my wits clear. Don't let my feelings of injustice rule my reason.*

Grandpa George shook the law officer's hand. "Mighty nice day we have for ourselves. No sign of a duster in sight. Out for a little ride, Sheriff?"

How did he remain so calm? Grandpa showed more grace than this man deserved.

"Well, now. I just wanted to stop by and see how the harvesting is going. Or not. I hear you may be in foreclosure soon if you can't pay off the mortgage." The sheriff surveyed the fields with calculating eyes. "If nothing happens, you should have a bountiful crop for the sugar factory. When do you plan to flood the fields?"

"Tomorrow, we'll open up the gates. Give it a day or two. Don't worry, Sheriff, I'll have the money just in time to pay off Hamilton. It'll be close."

"And you, Mr. Dettmann. How are you, today? Digging any more irrigation ditches?"

"No, been working on making spud cellars for some of the folks who grew potatoes. Looks like a decent amount of taters were harvested now that homesteaders can get some water to their fields. Next year, if it rains, they won't even need to irrigate."

"Well, well, well. You have been really busy making sure that the farmers can keep their land."

"Don't want the auctioneer to have more work than he can handle." Jess grinned.

"You let me decide how much the auctioneer needs to do. Well, thanks for the tour. I hope to see you soon." The sheriff scanned the fields one more time before he returned to his squad car.

"Stay in touch." Grandpa snarled the words between his teeth. Under his breath, he mumbled, "Love your enemies. Do good to those who despitefully use you."

Jess nodded to Grandpa George to affirm his thoughts. "Let's check the gates and get everything ready for tomorrow morning. The temperature is just about perfect, not too hot or too cold. We should be able to get into the fields without difficulty. Do we have enough help?"

"There are several families that live near Greeley who come from Mexico each year for the harvesting of the fields. The laborers we hired in the spring to help with the thinning went back home. I got in contact with Mr. Garcia last month and told him I would get in touch when we needed their help. There are maybe ten men who can join us."

Grandpa George had been busy. "Maybe we should go over there and confirm the plans and their wage rate. It will give all of us a clearer picture of what we are doing." Jess led the way to the green pick-up.

The sight of blue sky hugging the mountains always invigorated him. The rugged beauty of the mountains reminded him that God's bigger plan made the challenges of life worthwhile. Jess thought of Addy as she taught in the rural school for script, and the injustice of work with no paycheck. He admired her perseverance and ability to meet the difficulties that the eighth grade boys had created. Addy would make some man a good wife, he reflected. He creased his brow.

The road led through sand dunes taller than the top of his pick-up. Tumbleweeds piled on a fence line which was left over from a time when cattle still found clumps of grass for feed. Now, prairie dogs dug intricate towns that threatened to break the leg of any horse ridden in the area. Rattlers slithered up and down the sand piles in their quest for a meal. Eagles circled overhead in search of a stray rodent. Man's attachment to the land was an amazing thing.

It took a while to find the small adobe houses clustered together on the edge of town. Built many years before, the occupants kept the trash picked up and planted a few pots of flowers. Their care extended even to the outside ovens and heavy pots hanging over open fires. The aroma of spicy chili and baking bread reminded Jess's stomach that he had not eaten since an early breakfast.

"Over there." Grandpa George pointed to an older man who carved a piece of wood with a small knife while he sat on a three-legged stool. "That is Mr. Garcia. He is the one who organizes the crews to work in the fields."

Jess parked the pick-up, and they sauntered over to Mr. Garcia. He lay his whittling down. Grandpa George shook his hand.

"This is my right hand man, Jess Dettmann. He will be helping with the heavy work in the fields along with your men, if you don't mind."

Mr. Garcia removed his straw hat and held it near his chest. "I am happy to meet you, Mr. Dettman."

They greeted each other with a hand shake.

"I must tell you my bad news."

Jess held his breath. Now, what? Could anything else in life fall apart?

"I know that we had an agreement to hire out to you at the time of harvest." Mr. Garcia hesitated as he glanced at his feet, then made eye contact with Grandpa George. "Several men came to my house last week and told me that it would not be good for my family or those in our group if we worked your fields." The man sighed. "I want no trouble. I am very sorry."

The women, wearing long skirts, worked on looms or cooked on open flames. The sounds of children playing behind the building filled the air with carefree voices. These people possessed no protection or way to stand up to the intimidation of Hamilton's henchmen. He couldn't blame them for trying to get through the harvest time with homesteads that the bank wanted for auction. Bullying. It was everywhere and worked to make people afraid to do what was right. His fingernails dug deep into his palms.

He recalled being trapped by people in power and having no recourse. His muscles tensed, fists clenched. His mind shaded like the landscape when dark dust clouds plumed in the sky with their deadly advance. *How long, Lord? How long?*

"I understand, Mr. Garcia. The Lord will provide." Grandpa's soft spoken words carried concern and gentleness. "Thank you for being honest with me. Now, you be safe. And your family. I won't cause any trouble. Let's head back, Jess."

Taking in a gulp of air before speaking, Jess cleared his throat. "Take care, Mr. Garcia." Jess turned with Grandpa George and drove back to the homestead in silence. The weight of the situation smothered their words.

By the time they returned to the homestead, Addy, RiverLyn, and Billy were already preparing supper. The children set the table and ran outside, grabbing their ball, bat, and mitts on the way. Jess took a short stroll to the irrigation ditch gates to be sure that everything was set for the morning release of water. The ditches had allowed drip watering of the beet roots during the dry summer. Tomorrow would be the first flooding of the fields. As Jess strode back to the house, the sun blazed bright, the beet leaves waved in the breeze, and the soil smelled fresh.

Jess returned to the farm house's porch where Grandpa George sat on a wooden crate, leaning on the outer wall. "Everything's ready."

"Don't tell Addy anything." Grandpa George whispered to Jess. "She has enough to worry about with that class of hers. God will take care of us."

Jess nodded. He had to find a way to help Grandpa George. *Lord, we need You to give us guidance tomorrow as we flood the fields. Help us in this harvest.*

Jess entered the house and leaned against the kitchen wall. He watched Addy as she peeled and thinly sliced potatoes on the cutting board. Her long, delicate fingers worked the knife with efficiency. Why did he think that she couldn't cook? "How did your day of teaching go?"

Addy minced an onion. His eyes watered from the onion's spray. He wiped a tear running down his cheek.

Addy chuckled. "Those eighth grade boys are really putting on the steam to catch up for several years of doing nothing. It's hard for them to stay focused all the time, and they want to slip back into laziness, but I just have to encourage them to get them back on task. Maybe they needed someone to reassure them. Seems like they get a lot of demands and discouragement from their folks."

She plopped a spoon of lard into a big iron skillet. Once it sizzled, she put the potatoes and onions in to fry.

When she threw in cut-up chunks of Sunday's left-over beef roast, Jess's stomach growled at the aroma. "Hamilton would be a hard man to have as a father. Seems that nothing that his son does can measure up to his expectations. It's frustrating to try to please people who can't ever be satisfied with anything but perfection."

"I just remembered something that my grandmother told me when we were cooking."

"Grandma Martha was filled with wisdom."

"She took an egg and a potato and put them in a pan of boiling water. 'That's life,' she said. 'Same circumstances in life make one person bitter and the other compassionate, just like this boiling water makes the egg hard and the potato soft. What you are comes out in the heat of difficulty. Now, you be a potato, Addy.'" Taking the rim of her apron, Addy wiped a tear he suspected didn't come from the onions.

Jess grinned as warmth filled his chest. *I'll never think of potatoes the same.*

Addy's voice softened. "My grandmother expressed unconditional love to me. I guess I'm just realizing how precious a gift she gave to me. Wish that my mother could have seen Grandpa and Grandma's love that way."

Grandpa George opened the screen door just a sliver. "Mm. That smells good, Addy. You fry up leftovers just like Martha did. I'll go get the kids. Those spuds are just about done."

"I hear tell you are going to flood the fields tomorrow." Addy scooped the crispy, fried potatoes into a large bowl. "Would you get the jello out of the refrigerator?"

He took the bowl of green gelatin loaded with cut up cabbage and carrots from the refrigerator and placed it on the table. "We will be flooding, yes." He reached into the silverware drawer, pulled out a serving spoon, and stuck it into the jello.

The flooding was the easy part. Just open up the gates, and let the water flow. The rest seemed nearly impossible. How would they be able to harvest all those beets was beyond him.

The door creaked open. RiverLyn, Billy, and Grandpa strolled to the table.

RiverLyn sat down between Grandpa George and Billy. "We washed up at the pump."

"My favorite. Fried potatoes with meat. This is a good day." Billy breathed in the aroma of food like a boy who hadn't eaten since lunch.

"And it ain't from a can," Grandpa George muttered.

Everyone laughed.

After dinner, when the dishes were washed and dried, Grandpa George and the children huddled in the corner to listen to the Sons of the Pioneers singing "Tumbling Tumbleweeds" on the radio. Addy brought out her quilting materials and set them on the clean table.

"So, which square are you working on tonight?" Jess picked up a finished piece. "Your stitches are uniform and neat. Just like my own mother might have sewn if she hadn't succumbed to dust pneumonia at the beginning of the black blizzards." He paused, feeling the texture of the fabric between his fingers. "But she lived long enough to know that I was a pastor in a church, and it meant a lot to her."

The clucking of chickens from outside filled the silence. "It was a blessing that Father passed away before my problems became newspaper copy." He laid the quilt squares on the table. "Well, meeting Albert and Calvin got me to thinking about all the folks who have been displaced by the dusters. Seems to me that there should be a square to remind me of my job, and how my needs have been met day by day."

"Look." Addy held up a scrap of navy blue fabric. "This piece of cloth is from the young woman seated outside a Hooverville shanty. She was working on a quilt with the tiniest stitches I have ever seen." She pointed to a light blue and white thin striped feed-sack cloth that lay on the table. "She gave me that piece of striped material for Overall Sam's shirt. I've been saving these scraps for just this particular square. Hmm. I will make a straw hat to complete his outfit."

Rummaging in the pile of fabrics, Addy pulled out a small remnant of checked orange and yellow fabric. "What do you think?"

"I think this is going to be a really special quilt. I like this square because it's made up from things the people of Hooverville shared. Overall Sam will remind me of how fortunate I have been to live in the log cabin here on Grandpa George and Grandma Martha's homestead when being homeless is the fate of so many. Yep. It's going to be a special square." It would help him to recall a day with a pretty teacher who showed compassion for those less fortunate.

Jess enjoyed the cozy setting by the table as Addy picked up her scissors to cut the Overall Sam pattern. In the background, the radio waves brought the music of the Sons of the Pioneers as they strummed their guitars and howled for "Cool Water".

Water. The harvesting of beets depended on a good soaking to release the bulbs from the soil in undamaged condition. But how could he and an old man pick acres and acres of beets in a matter of hours? Grandpa George would lose the farm if they didn't at least try to do it.

Chapter 16

Morning sunshine pouring in the school house windows flickered off the dust particles floating in the air. The clock on the wall signaled time for class to start. Addy spot checked for absent students. Only one empty seat, which was good for the attendance at this time of the year when students helped their folks with the harvesting of crops. Since the drought started several years ago, the number of pupils present in school increased as children weren't needed for planting, thinning, weeding, or harvesting. The down side meant less to eat for everybody.

"Lillian is not here. Does anyone know if she is sick?" *Please, God, don't let her have dust pneumonia. I couldn't bear to have another child sick with that suffocating condition.*

Merle Murphy spoke up. "Beg your pardon, Miss Meyers. Lillian and her family done moved yesterday. After the auction at Goodwill homestead, they don't want to jest keep tryin' to hold onto a mortgage they can't pay. Anyways, that's what my ma told me."

Several students glanced in Harry's direction. His cheeks blazed as he stared at the black board with the eighth grade math homework posted on it.

Merle nodded his head toward the back of the room.

A hush settled over the class.

RiverLyn squirmed in her seat.

"My pa said that it's people like the Hamiltons who are robbing the farmers and the ranchers. Those folks don't have nuthin', then the bank even takes that. My ma says that Harry's pa all but stole the squeak from the pig when he foreclosed on Matt's farm. You don't know Matt because he was here last year before his family packed up a Ford to go to California."

Merle stood. "You're rich, Harry, because you rob from the poor." As he spoke, Merle turned to the back of the room. He pointed his finger straight at Harry.

All students focused their attention on the two boys.

Merle Murphy, the accuser.

Harry Hamilton, the accused.

"Take it back, Merle." Harry spoke in a calm voice through pressed lips. "I'm not my father." Harry's face burned red with each word.

"I won't take it back, 'cause you know deep down that it's true." Merle appealed to his classmates. "Ain't it?"

"Yeah."

"Your pa's a thief, Harry, and you're jest like yer old man."

"The bank is out to git us."

"My pa carries a lead pipe with him when he goes to the auctions."

"Git him, Merle!"

Harry stood to his full height. Claude and Melvin rose in unison with him.

Blood rushed to the top of Addy's head, producing a headache. She breathed in just as Merle leapt over the long table and bench. In seconds, he bounded in front of Harry, who stepped out from behind the table. The two boys fisted their hands.

Harry's solid shoulders loomed above Merle's small frame. But Merle shot up and caught Harry in the jaw. Harry sunk onto the floor, his nose leaking blood onto his shirt. Bouncing up and down like a boxer, Merle kept his fists at chest level.

Addy raced forward. "Get a cloth for me, Billy."

Once she reached Harry, Billy handed her a clean cloth from the supply closet. She placed it over Harry's nose to stop the bleeding. "Hold your head back. It will help the blood to clot."

Harry did as instructed and leaned over until he almost lay on the floor. Claude and Melvin flashed menacing stares at the other students. Nobody moved.

"You gonna let Merle git away with hittin' Harry like that?" Claude moved close to Addy. Melvin knelt by Harry.

"Merle, go back to your seat. Melvin and Claude, take Harry outside to the pump and put some cold water on his face. Try to wash him off a bit. Billy, get them more cloths." Addy smoothed her skirt to keep her hands from shaking. "Boys and girls, we need to get back to our work. Everyone take out your slates and copy your math problems from the board. I need to speak to Merle, so do your best to work on your own."

Some of the younger girls whimpered and cried. RiverLyn consoled them. "It's alright. Miss Meyers will make everything okay."

How could she make this okay? It happened so fast she didn't have time to respond. What kind of teacher was she to allow a fight in the classroom? What would Mr. Hamilton do when he found out about this?

Addy placed two small chairs in the back of the room, on the opposite side of the eighth grade boys' table. She motioned Merle to join her in a semi-private corner. He dragged his feet on the wooden floor and refused eye contact. Several tears rolled down his cheeks, but he wiped them with the back of his hand.

In Addy's perspective, those tears meant he was sorry for what he did. She was just glad that Harry didn't hit him back. What would cause Merle to lash out like that? Addy patted the chair seat next to her, and

Merle sat on it. The room quieted so much that Addy thought she heard an ant crawling on a lard bucket. She leaned in, close to Merle. "Tell me what just happened."

Merle's shoulders shook. Then he spoke in a subdued voice. "I ain't as old as those boys, and my ma and pa don't have a lot of fancy things. Most people I know don't. But what we got is our respect, Miss Meyers. I see parents workin' themselves every day to try to feed us kids, and then they git treated so bad. It ain't fair what's goin' on. With Lillian or anyone else. I hear the adults talkin' and things are heatin' up."

And with another auction or foreclosure coming up, there would be more emotional outbursts from the homesteaders around the Big Thompson River Basin. Somehow, Grandpa and Jess had to get the beet harvest in to get the money for the bank.

If only she got paid in cash and not in script.

# # #

Jess paced himself as he walked to gate three which would release water into the main irrigation ditch, using gravity to flood the subsidiary ditches and flood the beet fields. This part of the harvest he understood well, because he had spent time designing and digging each ditch. Water systems were something he understood. People sometimes puzzled him.

Why did men like those on the church board or like Hamilton want to bully other people? He kicked the dirt as he continued walking toward the wooden gate. Taking off his hat, he stared into the sky. "God, I don't know what to do. Grandpa George needs help, and I just don't know how to help him. Give me the faith that I need for this task. I don't even have enough for a mustard seed, and You promised that those with even that amount could move mountains. Give me faith the size of a grain of dust that falls from the clouds. I come in desperation." He jammed his hat onto his head.

Quickening his strides, he covered ground. He reached the gate, and gazed at a trickle of muddy water flowing toward the intake area. Where was the water? How could they flood the fields if there was no water? He followed the path of the trickle, hoping to get to the source of the problem. Acre after acre, the main irrigation ditch produced no more than a mere stream. Finally, he headed back to the homestead, running the last half mile.

"Are you back so soon? Got the fields flooded that fast?" Grandpa George peeled potatoes for supper.

"We've got a problem." Jess breathed with heavy gasps.

Grandpa George laid down the paring knife. "What now?"

"There is no water flowing into the irrigation ditch from the Big Thompson River. Must be a blockage somewhere on the river upstream. We have to find it and remove it so the water can flow."

"Here, Jess." Grandpa George shuffled over to the table with a pot of coffee. "Drink some of this, and then we'll have supper. Addy and the kids will be coming soon." He poured the dark brew into a mug on the table.

"You're so calm. I am tired of men like Hamilton lording it over everyone else just because he has some cash. How do you stay so centered?" Jess grasped the mug's handle until his fingers ached.

"It's taken a lot of time and a lot of hardship for me to realize that we are in God's hands. We can do what we need to do, but in the end, God will have His say. I have come to peace with the fact that this farm may go into foreclosure." Grandpa George diced an onion for the potato dish. "But I also know that God has plans for Addy and those kids. He knows that we need this homestead. It is better to rest in God's arms than to try and fight Him."

Jess was the pastor of a church, and, yet, this man exhibited more faith that God was in control of everything. *Lord, help me now to trust You in finding the source of the blockage of the irrigation system.* Jess sipped more coffee. The brew slid down his throat and perked him up. He needed to be alert and clear thinking.

God, help my unbelief.

# # #

An unnatural quiet hung in the schoolhouse. A hazy cast filled the air. Claude and Melvin flanked Harry as they stepped back into the one room rural school. Taking out their slates, they worked on the math problems chalked on the board. The silence and coughing caused Addy to grind her teeth.

The afternoon dragged like a heavy chest across a sand dune. The younger students made a paper chain to hang on the front of Addy's desk. The older pupils circled Merle like a wagon train. The eighth graders hunkered in and worked. Although the moments of the day stretched like an eternity to Addy, at last the clock ticked three on the dot.

She sighed. "If Merle and Harry will remain seated, the rest of the class is dismissed until tomorrow."

The children grabbed their lard buckets and bolted for the door. Sauntering behind the younger students, Claude and Melvin glanced over their shoulders at Harry, who sat on his bench and leaned back onto the wall. A red stain on the front of his shirt and the puffiness of his nose attested to the morning's struggle. Harry folded his arms across his chest.

Merle's shoulders shook as he hunched in his seat. She walked to him. "Do you have anything to say to Harry?"

Merle swiped at his eyes.

Harry shifted his weight. He focused his attention on Merle.

Standing, Merle made eye contact with Harry. "I'm sorry for the nose bleed. But I ain't sorry for what I said. It's the truth. I had no right to punch you for your pa's deeds."

"Oh, great. That's not taking responsibility for actions, Merle. What you're saying is true, but we need an apology here. A real one." Addy groaned. "I don't want to be involved in some kind of feud between the Murphys and the Hamiltons."

"You've got guts, kid. Hardly anyone stands up to my father." Harry stretched out his hand to Merle. "I've heard worse things about the bank and what's going on from the folks in town. Criticism comes with being a Hamilton. No hard feelings?"

Merle squinted, then glanced at Addy. She nodded.

"We can't be friends. But we don't need to be enemies." Merle reached out, and the boys shook.

She took a deep breath. "Okay, boys. Go on home. Merle, you go out first, then Harry will follow. I don't want you two walking home together."

Merle grabbed his lard bucket. "Bye, Miss Meyers."

Harry smiled at Addy. "This has been a day to remember. I get punished for being a Hamilton all the time, but I want to do something to make a mark on this world. Just me. Not on my father's name."

"I believe you will do that, Harry. Go right home, now."

"Okay, Miss Meyers. Have a pleasant evening." Harry waved over his shoulder.

RiverLyn and Billy tiptoed into the room.

Bill exhaled. "Guess it's safe now."

"Let's get this place cleaned. I'll start putting up tomorrow's board work. Billy, sweep the floor. RiverLyn, move some of this dust outside where it belongs." Addy erased the board as she spoke.

She just finished covering the black slate with new work when the low hum of an automobile's motor reached her. A car door slammed. Heavy footsteps pounded the stairs. The door flew open.

Mr. Hamilton, president of the bank and head of the school board, stood in the door's frame.

"You children. Go outside, and wait until we're done." Hamilton pointed outside. RiverLyn and Billy scuttled past him.

"You are in big trouble, Miss Meyers. I don't want to hear your side of any story that you concoct. Harry told me what happened. Since you have no control over these children, I am putting you on report. Tomorrow, I will teach this school. You will stay home. The board meeting is next evening. We will decide what to do with you then. Get your purse, or whatever you women carry, and get out of here."

Addy's heart pounded. He couldn't do that, could he? Was Hamilton firing her? What would she do with the script? Could she turn it in and help out Grandpa? How would they buy food if she lost this job?

Addy grabbed her bag of papers to be corrected along with her lard bucket and slunk out the door like a naughty child put in her place. RiverLyn and Billy raced in the classroom and picked up their lunch pails. The three trudged home in silence.

As they passed the first stand of tumbleweeds, a car roared away in the opposite direction. Addy turned. The dust cloud from Hamilton's vehicle disappeared behind a sand dune.

What would she say to Grandpa?

The threesome walked into the yard. The aroma of potatoes and onions wafted from the wind-scarred wooden house. Comfort food. Exactly what she needed tonight. She scurried with RiverLyn and Billy the few feet to the porch stairs. They all burst through the doorway at the same time.

"Whoa. Slow down, there. I still run a civilized house here." Grandpa scooped the last of the spuds into a large bowl, which he set on the table. "Wash up, and then we'll chow down."

Jess pulled the corn on the cob from the water and placed the ears on a platter. He winked at Addy. "Glad to see you back home again."

Her cheeks warmed in response. "It's been a long day."

After the prayer, all dug in. For several moments, the room sounded like it was full of young pigs at a trough as they chomped into succulent ears of corn.

"Addy has bad news." Billy spoke with his mouth overflowing with yellow kernels.

RiverLyn wiped the corn juice on her mouth with her napkin. "Really bad." She drew the words out long, with an air of drama.

Jess and Grandpa stopped chewing. A hush fell over the table.

"Well." Grandpa broke the silence.

"Well, what?" Addy glared at Billy.

"What's yer bad news?"

Addy choked back tears. Her heart ached as she gasped for air. The stillness in the room suffocated her. "Mr. Hamilton canceled school for me. He's going to teach the children. I go before the board tomorrow night to get fired."

"Fired?" Grandpa struck the table with a poof of dust and clatter of dishes.

Jess pushed his chair back. "Is this legal? Can he do this to her?"

Addy shook her head. "He is president of the school board. There are few bylaws to that position. Any bully can wield power. I saw it in Topeka."

"I'm tired of the intimidating, aggressive men making the lives of others miserable." Jess pulled his chair close to the table and shoved his fork into his pile of fried potatoes. "We'll see what happens at that school meeting. Confronting groups of power-grubbing men is my specialty." He bit into a mouthful of comfort food.

Addy and Grandpa exchanged looks while RiverLyn and Billy stared at Jess. Whoever imagined he had that much fight in him?

"What did you do to make him so mad?" Grandpa asked.

"It wasn't her fault." Billy wiped his hands on his shirt tail. "Lillian and her family moved away because of owing money to the bank, and Merle got mad about it 'cause his folks know all these farmers who are losin' their land. Merle talked to Harry like he had somethin' to do with it, but Harry don't know how to take over farms. It's his pa that everyone hates."

Grandpa rubbed his chin for a moment. "So, what does this disagreement have to do with Addy?"

"You're tellin' it all wrong. You didn't tell them about the fight. That's why Addy can't teach tomorrow." RiverLyn pointed her fork at Billy.

"I told it right. Just give me a chance to get to the good part."

Addy gulped. "Good part?"

"Yeah, when Merle jumped over all the tables and hit Harry. Pow! Blood all over from that big nose of Harry's. Sure got him by surprise." Billy's eyes shone.

"All of us. Merle caught all of us by surprise. I don't know a much smaller boy could do so much harm to someone so much larger. But he did. And after school, I guess his parents saw his bloody shirt and puffy nose, and that's when Mr. Hamilton drove to the school to tell me to take the day off. He sure looked mad."

"Oh." Jess chuckled. "Hamilton's angry at all of us for a lot of reasons. Wouldn't you agree, Grandpa?"

Grandpa snapped his fingers. "That reminds me, Addy. We will need some help tomorrow."

"Did you flood the fields? Can we start harvesting some of the beets? I can do my share."

"That's the problem. Jess went to open the water gate, and only a trickle poured in. Not enough to wet the roots. He thinks there is a blockage somewhere upstream that will need to be removed."

Billy stood up. "Can I go, Jess? Can I help you do that?"

Jess glanced at Grandpa, then Addy. "You will be needed here on the homestead. I can handle moving a few rocks that might have fallen in the foothills. It's a one-man job."

"I never git to do anything but stay at home." Billy scowled.

"I could go along and help." The words popped out of Addy's mouth before she thought of what it meant. Alone in the foothills with Jess. This was a day to throw caution to the wind and follow her heart.

"First, let me investigate the main ditches to discover where the breach occurred. I need to verify if the blockage is from natural causes, or man-made."

"Man made?"

"With water rights at stake on a homestead, some people are desperate enough to go outside the law to get the property they want. That's why I'll go alone. If your help is needed, I'll be back for you." Jess glanced at the dish drain. "I can dry the dishes before turning in."

"No, you have to get up early in the morning. Grandpa and I will have the kitchen clean in no time." She started to stack the silverware by the sink.

Jess waved before opening the screen door and heading for bed.

"Now, you kids need to git some shut-eye too. Off with you." Grandpa waved toward the hall entrance.

Billy groaned loud and long. RiverLyn yawned. Then they dragged themselves to their bedrooms.

Grandpa took the wash cloth from Addy. "Now, you need to git some sleep if'n you face those low snakes in the grass tomorrow night. Got to have yer senses about ya."

"I let everyone down. How will the farm be saved if I am fired and can't cash in my script?"

"Child, did you think that the future of this here farm rested on yer shoulders? No, sir. I am the one responsible to pay this debt, not you. I trust the Lord will do what's right by me. So, git some shut-eye."

"Oh, I can't relax. I'm going to work on the quilt. Just two more squares to create, then I can stitch the top together. The sewing will relax me." Addy kissed Grandpa's cheek.

She gathered her sewing kit, laying out the materials on the kitchen table as Grandpa finished the dishes. An owl hooted from the barn, the only sound beside the wind blowing gravel. There were all the finished quilt squares: Billy, RiverLyn, the photographer, Grandma Martha, Katrina, the hobo, and one of herself.

From the scrap pile, Addy found black material for Overall Sam's body. Gray for the hat. As she appliquéd the design onto the white muslin square, she visualized the man who wore suits and lived what he believed. A man who lived in a way of living that was different from anyone she knew. A man able to capture her thoughts all day and all night.

By the time the moon hung high in the sky, she finished stitching a Bible in the hand of Overall Sam. Or Jess Dettmann. Addy's muscles relaxed she held the finished block.

One more square to make. In many ways, an important one. Maybe the hardest one, which is why she procrastinated making it. Grandpa. How could she possibly make an Overall Sam that would be worthy of all the love and protection the gray-haired man gave her over the years?

With trepidation, she chose fabric from Grandpa's pants and cut out the framework of a body. An old shirt still had a section of the back in good condition, so she outlined a shirt for her appliquéd figure. Autumn-gold felt served as Grandpa's straw hat. Addy pulled the needle one more time, created a knot, and sliced the thread. The deep colors of the quilt square fit Grandpa's defiant approach to hardship.

Chapter 17

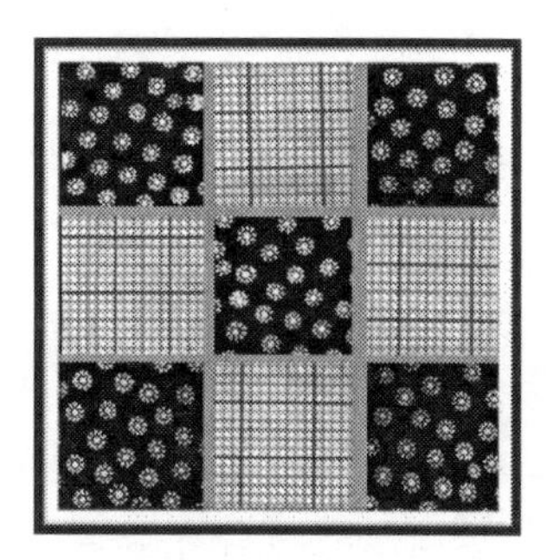

As autumn morning sun poured into the kitchen, Addy stood at the stove stirring the oatmeal. Billy and RiverLyn played ball tag outside while Grandpa finished the chores. The screen door opened with a gust of wind and Jess entered.

"I found it. I found where those henchmen of Hamilton blew up some rocks on the mountain side. The rocks are in the head of the main irrigation ditch coming off the Big Thompson River." Jess breathed like a man who ran a marathon.

"Sit down and have a cup of coffee." Addy poured a mug full of java.

"Did you find the blockage?" Grandpa walked into the kitchen. "Pour me a cuppa joe, too, if ya don't mind."

"It will take a while to clear the rocks, but it is possible. Thank goodness, the job I was working on two days ago is near there. Moving a dragline is a slow process, so it's good we're close."

"Can I go with you?" Addy brought the oatmeal pan to the table and scooped out portions for each bowl.

Jess's eyes brightened. "It isn't comfortable in a dragline, but you may be helpful in deciding the sequence of which rocks to move."

RiverLyn and Billy bounded in the door and scooted their chairs close to the table.

"Do we have to go to school today?" Billy jammed his mouth with oatmeal.

"Don't even think different." Grandpa lifted his spoon. "We need you two children to tell us how Hamilton does as a teacher. Just sit quiet and watch."

RiverLyn giggled as she scooped another mouthful of creamy oatmeal. "Oh, this will be fun. We'll be like spies or secret agents."

Addy sighed. "Be sure to be respectful. Don't give Hamilton any ammunition for tonight."

"Don't worry." Billy grabbed his lard bucket. "Let's go, RiverLyn."

The door slammed.

"I'll tidy up the kitchen while you head out to clear the ditch." Grandpa stood, then walked to the sink with a stiff gait. "Just need to get the kinks out in the morning."

Jess drove the green Ford pick-up on dirt lanes that ran parallel to the gates of the irrigation ditches. Dry furrows in the ground, these ditches needed to be filled with water by afternoon if the beets were to be harvested in time. Soon, the vehicle bumped over cow paths that led to the dragline sitting beside a spud cellar.

"Well, here we are." Jess crossed over to the big machine. "Old Betsy." He patted the metal wheel. "Let me help you into the cab."

Addy stepped on the top of the wheel, then leaned on his shoulder. With a push, she propelled into the cab. Enough room for one operator, a cozy space for two.

Jess climbed in and settled on the seat close to her. The touch of his shoulder pressed against her sent shivers up and down her spine. He started the motor and rolled the machine onto the flat bed of a truck. She watched as he worked all the controls and levers to place the dragline onto the trailer. What a great amount of dexterity it took to maneuver such a piece of equipment.

"Okay, hop down, and we'll ride in the truck cab." Jess held out his hand when he landed on the dusty plains, and caught her around her waist. Gently, he lowered her onto the land, close to his body. Close enough for her to feel his breath on her neck. She wanted to melt into his arms, but she pulled back.

Addy climbed into the cab of the large truck, Jess taking his seat on the driver's side. Within seconds, the truck lurched forward as it pulled the heavy load on the trailer. The vehicle moved along the dirt road toward higher altitude. As the road reached its crest, Jess touched Addy's arm.

"We'll be going downhill for a bit. I want you to stand on the running board."

"Why?" She glanced out the window, at the steep drop off.

"If this truck loses its brakes, you'll need to jump off."

"What about you?" She swallowed hard.

"I'll jump if I get a chance. Now, open your door, and hang on."

Addy pulled the lever on the metal door. It creaked open. She stood on the running board, and hung onto the door frame. The truck crawled downhill, the smell of burning rubber filling Addy's nostrils.

"There it is." He pointed to a pile of rocks near a river bed and applied the brakes. "Now, if you can guide me and my machine off the trailer, it would be a great help."

She used hand signals to help him steer Old Betsy off the flat bed. He waved for her to climb onto the dragline. She snuggled close to him in the cab as he steered the dragline to the pile of rocks. An overflow of water dampened the drought-ridden soil behind the boulders. A trickle of water slid down the foothill.

Addy clenched her fists. "It is so evident there wasn't a landslide here. That dam on the drainage ditch is the result of explosives in the hands of man."

"Old Betsy will take care of those boulders in no time at all." He eased the bucket of the dragline over the top rock. With skill, he moved it off the pile and onto the side. By cherry picking each obstacle, he freed the water so it ran in the main irrigation feeder ditch. The trench filled with water, flowing briskly toward the lower altitude of the plains.

They loaded Old Betsy onto the flat bed. When the engine was turned off, Addy realized how loud it had been. The peace of the nature around her relaxed the tightened muscles in her back.

"Well," he sighed, "let's head out to the homestead."

They climbed back into the truck. Again, she stood on the running board as the vehicle rolled down the foothills to the plains.

When they got to the spud cellar, she moved to the driver's seat of the pick-up and led the caravan of vehicles and equipment to Grandpa George's homestead. Being able to work side-by-side with Jess filled her with joy. She parked by his cabin and waited until he eased the truck and trailer into place.

Together they walked to each of the gates of the irrigation ditches. As he opened them one-by-one, she clapped her hands as the water flowed into the furrows alongside the beets, soaking their roots, making it possible to harvest the crop. In another day, pulling up the beets would be possible.

They held hands as they strolled back to the house. They burst into the kitchen.

Nothing prepared them for the scene. Addy stopped short, her breath catching in her throat.

Grandpa lying on the floor, a broken mug of coffee staining the wood floor.

Addy slumped beside him. "Grandpa. Grandpa. Please say something to me."

As she spoke, Grandpa's eyes fluttered. "Addy. Don't worry."

Jess crouched on the other side. "Do you hurt anywhere? What happened?"

"I'll git up when the world stops spinning." Grandpa closed his eyelids. "Can't keep my eyes open. That's when everything spins the fastest."

"Vertigo. He has vertigo. Complete bed rest is the only cure." Jess exhaled.

"How do you know?" She stared at the unmoving body of her grandfather.

"I've seen it in the camps. Don't know how a person gets vertigo, but lying perfectly still is the best way to treat it." Jess lifted Grandpa. "Let me get you to your bed."

She followed as Jess led Grandpa to his metal-framed bed. She pulled back the comforter and sheet, took off Grandpa's boots, and tucked him into the coziness. "Now, rest." She kissed his cheek.

Jess and Addy huddled by the kitchen sink.

She whispered. "How long do you think he will have vertigo?"

"Hard to tell. Sometimes it lasts for a few days until the person is solid on their feet."

"That means one less person for the harvest."

"That may be a blessing in disguise for Grandpa George. He shouldn't be working so hard." Jess leaned close to Addy. Her breathing deepened as he spoke. "The group of workers that we counted on to help us have been intimidated by Hamilton and his crew.

"What are we going to do? How can we bring in all those beets in a day or two?"

"I have an idea. Let me work it out."

"This, on top of being worried about the board meeting tonight."

"You should be. Hamilton is going to throw everything he's got at you so you are fired and he can delay paying your script until after the debt money is due from Grandpa George." Jess spoke in a conversational tone. "Just keep a level head. Don't let Hamilton play on your emotions. He's counting on you folding up like an accordion and crying. It will make you look weak and ineffective. That's just the image he wants."

"He doesn't know me that well, then. It takes more than a surly bully to make me cry." All those years in Topeka as a child when the big boys on the block teased her made her tough.

"I need to do some business this afternoon, but I will be back in time to take you to the board meeting." He leaned and kissed her cheek. "Take care of Grandpa George and relax."

She stepped forward and stood on tiptoe. She drew him close and kissed him on the lips. He embraced her. The warmth of the moment filled her with desires she had not known existed.

She didn't feel tough. She melted like an ice cube in August.

# # #

The afternoon sun moved to the western sky above the mountains as RiverLyn and Billy burst through the door.

"Shhh!" Addy shushed the kids. "Grandpa is in bed."

RiverLyn's eyes widened. "Is he sick?"

"No, he is dizzy. It's a condition called vertigo. He needs to remain motionless until it clears up."

Billy hung up his school jacket and grabbed his barn coat. "I can do his chores for him."

"This family pulls together in times of need. That makes me happy." Addy's mother never knew how to handle difficulties. She just headed for a new man and a bottle. Grandpa built a spirit in these children that was worthwhile. She delighted in being part of that.

"You should have seen Mr. Hamilton today." RiverLyn shook her head. "He didn't know what he was doing. Nobody read the stories with the first and second graders. Hamilton couldn't figure out the math problems that the eighth graders were working on."

"Did you offer to help?"

RiverLyn shook her head. "Are ya' kiddin'? Let that man sweat. He needs to appreciate you."

Billy chuckled. "Hamilton looked tired at the end of the day. All the kids were talking out of turn and not doing their seat work. He yelled once, but it didn't do any good."

Addy wanted to cheer, but didn't. After all, the students were the ones who lost a day of learning that would need to be reclaimed. That meant extra work for her and them.

"RiverLyn, go in and talk with Grandpa. He probably won't open his eyes, but he would enjoy some company. Billy, feed the chickens, milk the cow, and bed down the horse. I'll make supper."

Perspiration beaded on Addy's brow. What if tonight was a disaster?

Chapter 18

Model T Fords, horses and buggies, as well as Hamilton's newest vehicle already crowded the open space around the school building. Jess pulled the pick-up to the fence line covered with tumbleweeds. Addy leaned on him for support as they navigated the parking lot of dust and dirt.

People packed the classroom, sitting on the benches, leaning on the walls. Hamilton seated himself in the teacher's chair behind her desk. Addy ground her teeth.

Within minutes, Hamilton and the school board henchmen stood in front of the blackboards.

"I'm calling this special meeting to order." Hamilton's voice boomed over the chattering crowd, which hushed on command. "Glad to see so many people interested in the education of their children."

Some may see a smile on that face, but that was a sneer. Addy straightened her spine. Her neck hairs bristled. Jess touched her shoulder, and the tension flowed out of her.

"Come up here, Miss Meyers, since you are the subject of the meeting this evening."

She pressed the flour sack material of her skirt. She held her body erect as she moved among the spectators to get to the front. Turning to face the crowd, she spotted Jess and his wide grin. The parents of her students, their faces solemn, their jaws set. Merle Murphy's dad gained eye contact with her, then nodded twice. Underarm sweat soaked her blouse.

Hamilton smacked his lips. "It has come to my attention that Miss Meyers has been slack in her duties as teacher. She allows the children way too much time at recess to play. Last week, she held an unsanctioned baseball game that lasted well into the afternoon."

The school board members frowned in unison.

"We cannot have this type of nonsense going on when our children need an education in these hard times. Wouldn't you agree?"

Silence hung in the classroom like the calm in the eye of a tornado.

"I sure nuf don't agree." Patrick Murphy's Irish brogue filled the space. "My boy, Merle, comes home ev'ry day plum full of ideas from school. He gits excited 'bout his learnin'. I say, keep the teacher."

The crowd mumbled.

"Now, let's not be hasty. The school board will vote on whether or not we think Miss Meyers is doing an adequate job."

The men leaning against the back wall stood up, then moved forward. Several board members adjusted their ties.

"Don't you think the teacher should get paid?" Jess directed his question to Hamilton.

The audience exchanged glances of disbelief with each other.

Murphy adjusted his stance. "Seems I'm the spokesman. Is what that Dettmann feller says true? Don't the teacher git paid?"

Hamilton smirked. "Of course, Miss Meyers is getting paid."

"In cash or script?" Jess stared right at the president of the school board.

The crowd leaned forward.

"She will be paid in script until the tax money is received and other bills are cared for. That is sound business practice."

"So, this here teacher is comin' ev'ry day for free?" Murphy glanced about the room. "She must have expenses jest like us. How many of you want to work for script?" Raising his hand, Murphy pointed around the room, then focused it on Hamilton. "Do you work fer script?"

Laughter filled the dusty room.

Hamilton hooded his eyes. "That's not the subject of this meeting. The board and I are worried about the quality of education that Miss Meyers provides."

Murphy stepped to the front of the room, standing next to Hamilton. Raising his hands in fists above his head, Patrick Murphy shouted. "All in favor of keepin' Miss Meyers as the teacher say 'aye.'"

The walls thundered with the reply.

Turning so he faced the school board, Murphy waited for silence before he asked. "Anyone object?"

The only sound was a lonely coyote crying to the moon.

"Then, the matter is settled. Everyone go home, because school will be in session on Monday morning. And Mr. Hamilton is gonna work on gittin' Miss Meyers some cash." Murphy nodded toward the president of the school board and head of the bank.

Cheers and applause fueled the audience as they headed for their rides home. Murphy stayed at Hamilton's side until the room cleared, except for Addy and Jess and the board members.

"You tell me if this big ox gives you any more trouble." Murphy winked at Addy, then strutted out the door.

"Don't think you have gained anything tonight." Hamilton snarled between clenched teeth. "Come on, men. Let's go back to my place and have a few drinks."

The school board followed Hamilton out the door. Murphy strutted behind them.

"Guess the teacher will close up her school." Jess pulled Addy into his arms. Her heart beat as fast as a jackrabbit being chased by a dog. "I've waited my whole life for a woman like you." His lips pressed on hers as she folded into his embrace.

When they arrived at the homestead, Billy and RiverLyn greeted them.

"Tell me all about it." Grandpa sat in an easy chair with his eyes closed. "I've been praying for you."

Between the two of them, Addy and Jess shared the events of the night.

"Now that you settled that, we need to git the beets harvested. Are the fields soaked?"

"Don't you worry, Grandpa George. I filled the irrigation ditches with water and have a plan for getting the harvest in before the debt is due." Jess patted the older man's shoulder.

Billy chimed in. "Do we git to help?"

"Of course. There is plenty of work for everyone. Addy and RiverLyn will be in charge of cooking for the harvesters. Billy, you will serve as our messenger between the field and homestead."

"But who's gonna harvest the beets?" Grandpa held his head steady as he spoke. The vertigo lingered. "Hamilton's crew of thugs scared off the usual farm workers."

"Oh, I know a whole group of people who need money and are willing to work. I stopped in Hooverville this afternoon. Calvin and the men have offered to harvest the beets. They want to go to California to work. This is an opportunity for these people to get out of Colorado before winter descends."

"How many plates will we need? How can I cook for a crowd?" The logistics of the menu overwhelmed Addy.

Jess rubbed his chin. "We can eat in shifts. Make a stew or casserole, baked beans, and buttered biscuits. Everyone loves jello. Calvin asked if some of the women could come to help out in the kitchen. Would you like that?"

"Yes, it might ease the load. Especially with the cooking. I know how to do dishes."

"Don't forget that I know how to help out." RiverLyn put her arm around Addy's waist.

"Then, let's git to bed. Tomorrow will be a big day." Jess helped Grandpa to his feet and steadied him as he shuffled to his bedroom.

# # #

Morning light burst into Addy's room. Her mental list of chores propelled her out of bed. She started soaking beans for cooking as a pot of coffee perked. By the time she brought out a pan of baking powder biscuits, the roll of tires on gravel sounded in the lane. RiverLyn, eyes still crusted from sleep, stirred a pot of oatmeal.

"Just in time. We can get a group of men eating and just keep rotating them in and out of the kitchen." Addy set the table for eight places with fresh milk in a pitcher from Billy's milking the cow.

Jess burst into the room with eight men trailing him. "Grandpa, stay in that chair. Here is the first group for breakfast, Addy. Send Billy with them to the irrigation gates, and he can bring back the next batch of eaters. Some womenfolk will be in to help."

Addy gestured toward the table and chairs. "Well, gentlemen, find a spot at the table, and we'll bring you some grub." The men wore tattered clothing. Their shoes barely held together. They removed their hats, then sat.

Calvin remained standing. A tear trickled on his cheek. "It's been a mighty long time since we all sat at a proper table. Thank you, God, for the blessing of this food and a job to do. Amen."

The men chorused, "Amen." Then they passed the biscuits and molasses while Addy dished out the oatmeal. Soon, coffee filled the mugs with fragrance and steam.

A knock at the door startled Addy.

Four women tiptoed into the kitchen, their eyes wide with wonder. Feed-sack bib aprons covered their flour-bag dresses. The trio pulled their hair back into severe buns at the napes of their necks. Addy's signal they wanted to get busy. She recognized Calvin's wife, Grace.

"Hi, I'm Addy. This here is RiverLyn. Does anyone know how to make biscuits? We are running out fast."

Grace spoke. "This is Ina, Viola, and Lois. We cook beans, casseroles, and stew meat the best. Just let us wash up and we'll git goin'."

Addy breathed her own prayer of thanksgiving for the help in the kitchen.

# # #

Jess needed to have breakfast, but decided to go with the second group of men. Calvin, his right hand man, could supervise the harvest while he ate. The men wanted to start the picking. They charged to the irrigation gates that Jess closed at early light.

Wet fields. Soaked soil. Perfect for pulling up the beets without damaging them.

"Calvin told us what to do, so we'll start now. Pair up, men. Does everyone have their beet hook?"

Each set of men headed for a long row of wet beets with a wheelbarrow or cart for them to fill with the harvest.

"Well, guess you and I will be working together, Tim. Which job are you most comfortable doing?" Jess stood at the beginning of a row that stretched for an acre.

"I have my beet hook and cart, so I'll follow you. Never thought I'd see a preacher harvesting a field."

"Never thought that I'd be harvesting with a musician." Jess chuckled. "I want to be close to the earth and the men who make a nation prosper. Guess that means I like ranchers and farmers."

Jess bent over and grabbed two beets by the green leaves. The bulbs slid from the damp soil. He knocked them together to shake free the dirt, then laid them in the row, tubers to one side, the greens to another.

Tim lifted the beet with one hand and chopped the crown and leaves with a single action from the beet hook. Then he placed the beet in the cart and repeated the procedure. Swish slid the knife. Clump into the cart. Swish. Clump. The morning sun rose higher in the sky. Jess's back ached.

Billy ran over to them with an empty cart. Then he dragged the full one to the pick-up truck. Several men who were emptying their wheelbarrows helped Billy load the beets onto the vehicle's bed. By the time the first crew finished breakfast, four pick-up beds overflowed with beets. Calvin and Jess drove two of the vehicles while two other men joined the caravan to the sugar refinery a half hour's drive down the road. The men who had been harvesting headed for breakfast, leaving four men to continue working the fields.

The Great Western Sugar Company refinery loomed above the flat land. The huge brick building with tall stacks billowing smoke ran its operation twenty-four hours a day during the brief season that the sugar beets matured. Tons of bulbous tubers created the sugar for the nation. These refineries dotted the northern Colorado foothills, close to the irrigated ranches.

Jess led the pick-ups to the weighing station, then to the unloading bins of the sugar refinery. He made sure every load bore the name of George Meyers. After they dumped the beets into the bins, each pick-up once again headed to the weigh station. The difference between the weights became the poundage credited. The staggering amount of work left to be done in Grandpa George's fields pressed on Jess like dark clouds roiling across the plains.

As the four pick-ups rolled onto the Meyers's homestead, Jess gazed at the unfamiliar horses tied near the watering tank, munching on hay.

Billy ran out of the house to greet him. "Ya'll never believe what jest happened, Jess."

"I suspect I can't guess, so you tell me."

"Patrick Murphy gathered up some ranchers and his kin. They're out harvesting beets right now."

Jess inhaled as he tried to soak in Billy's words. "Don't that beat all. I need to get out there."

"Tell a group of men to come back to the house for some chow. Addy and the women are fixin' up some fine food." Billy licked his chops.

Hurrying to the fields, Jess stared at the increased number of men scattered across the acreage, bending over the plants, hauling wheelbarrows and carts loaded with beets. Two trucks with large-capacity beds were parked at the head of the irrigation gates. A crew of men unloaded carts onto the trucks as soon as they pulled up to them.

Shading his eyes, Jess surveyed the men, spotting Patrick Murphy. He strode over to him. "I can't believe what I see."

"I was thinkin' at that meetin' last night that this here community needs to stick together 'ginst the bank. No more foreclosures. No more script. I left Ireland 'cause of injustice. Won't put up with it here." Murphy used his beet pick as he spoke, lobbing off the greenery from the bulb. Merle pushed the cart as fast as his father moved, processing the crop in an efficient manner.

"I'll join the fellas over there and keep the job going." Jess stepped over a few rows and joined several Hooverville men, including Tim. He pulled two beets at a time, knocked them together, then laid the cleaned vegetables on the ground. Tim followed Jess and chopped off the greenery.

Pull. Knock off the dirt. Lay down justice for Grandpa George and his debt payment.

Pull. Knock off the dirt. Lay down justice for Addy against the school board.

Pull. Knock off the dirt. Lay down justice for the homesteaders facing foreclosure.

Pull. Knock off the dirt. Lay down justice for the folks at Hooverville who want a second chance at life.

Pull. Knock off the dirt. Lay down justice for the orphan train riders who didn't find good homes.

Pull. Knock off the dirt. Lay down justice for Murphy and the immigrants scratching out a living.

Pull. Knock off the dirt. Lay down justice for himself. For the loss of his calling. For the pain he suffered.

Pull. Justice. Pull. Justice. The pace picked up.

Jess focused on the task of unearthing beets until the sun worked its way to the mountains. His arms ached, his back spit pain into his muscles, his stomach growled for food. He surveyed the nearly empty fields. With just a few rows left, the men harvested most of the beet crop in one long day.

A monumental task. One that Hamilton had not thought possible. Jess's sinews screamed in agony, but his spirit reveled in justice.

As the last carts and wheelbarrows unloaded their crop into the large trucks, Jess met with Murphy.

"I kin drive this rig to the sugar refinery with ya." Murphy dangled his keys.

"I'll take you up on that offer." Jess hopped onto the passenger seat of the truck.

The weary workers shuffled their feet in the direction of the house. Billy waved them into the light and smells of the kitchen. As the truck pulled away, Jess's mouth watered.

Weigh in. Unload. Weigh out. Collect the cash. Five hundred dollars. One thousand dollars.

The sun set. Two thousand dollars. Stars twinkled in the sky.

Then the last loads of beets were weighed. Three thousand eight hundred dollars.

Enough money to pay off the bank note. Enough to give wages to the workers. Maybe a start for next spring's planting.

Jess slumped in his seat as Murphy drove in the darkness, the headlights of his truck casting shadows on the sand piles close to the side of the road. Why had he ever doubted God's care?

The flickering glow of lights from the homestead warmed Jess's heart as the truck pulled in the yard. Two horses munching on bags of oats remained at the post. The only evidence of pick-ups and other vehicles were the deep tire prints in the dusty gravel.

The aroma of home cooking greeted the men as they entered the kitchen. Calvin and his wife sat talking with Grandpa George. Billy, RiverLyn, and Merle hunched over a Monopoly board on the ottoman. Addy used a large spoon to stir grub in an iron pot.

"Finally. You're here. I have some beans and biscuits. Hot coffee too. Sit down." The sweetness of her voice lifted his spirits despite his sore body. He hankered to come home to a woman like her.

Murphy and Jess plopped down on high-backed chairs, weariness overtaking them. The women dished up bowls of baked beans and placed a plate of golden bread in the middle of the table. The men joined them for coffee.

"How did we do?" Grandpa George sat but was careful not to turn too fast.

Placing a small stack of bills on the table, Jess whooped. "We made the money to pay off Hamilton."

A cheer resounded in the kitchen. Jess bit into a butter-laden bun dripping with molasses.

Jess counted out piles of five and ten dollar bills, then shoved the lot across the table. "Calvin, there is the cash for the men who worked. Murphy, for your kin and crew too."

Stomping of feet and shouts of "Alright!" filled the air for several minutes. Billy, Merle, and RiverLyn danced a jig. Addy wiped a tear from her eye. Jess stepped over and hugged her.

"I told the men to come here tomorrow to settle up. Your people, too, Murphy. It was gettin' late." Calvin grabbed a biscuit and stuffed it into his mouth.

"Besides, the women want to have a pot luck lunch tomorrow." Calvin's wife beamed as she brought more beans to the table in a bowl. "We have a lot to celebrate."

"Should I be baking something for the luncheon?" Addy sat beside Jess. Her nearness sped up the beat of his already-pounding heart.

"Just some biscuits and such. We'll set up an iron pot over a fire pit near your porch and have us a Hooverville stew." Grace poured coffee in her husband's mug.

Calvin blew on the deep, rich brew.

Addy asked, "How do you make Hooverville stew?"

"Everyone brings something to put into it. When the stew is mellow, then we eat." Grace carried coffee to the men.

Addy laughed. "Sounds like the old tale of stone soup."

"Exactly." Grace chuckled.

"I'll bring some fresh mutton meat and bones." Murphy raised a spoonful of beans to his lips. "The missus makes a tumbleweed salad that'll bring yer taste buds alive. Right, Merle?"

"She shore can, Pa."

Merle never missed a beat. Jess let a bite of biscuit melt in his mouth. Guess Hamilton and his son know that piece of fact about the Murphy family too.

As the owl hooted from the barn, Jess stepped outside with Patrick Murphy. "I can't thank you enough for what you have done for the Meyers."

"Never thought I'd work with a preacher. That makes me think about things." Gathering the reins on his horse, Murphy nodded his head. "Come mornin', I'll be here."

Chapter 19

There was so much to do early in the morning. Addy braced for the activities of the new day.

Grace offered to help her finish the quilt just before she left with Calvin late in the evening. Now, what was it Grace had told her to gather? She reached for the sewing basket with its quilt squares. She took a stack of washed and ironed sugar sack fabric from the top dresser drawer and a neatly-folded piece of cotton batting Grandpa found in the top of the closet. Needle. Thread. Guess that was all she needed.

Heading for the kitchen, she inhaled the aroma of fresh-perked coffee.

"Grandpa. You must be feeling better."

"Well, good 'nuf to sit up for the day. Billy helped me git to the table. He and Jess are doin' the chores. A feller could git used to this treatment."

"Let me pour a mug of coffee for you, and then get the oatmeal cooking." She tied Grandma's apron around her waist. *God, thank You for supplying the money for the farm. Thank you for all of the people who came to help. Your mercy has been shown to me in a special way. Amen.*

Addy spoke the words. The sounds of wheels grinding gravel caught her attention. Glancing out the window, she recognized trouble as it braked by the windmill.

"It's the sheriff and Hamilton. From the grumpy expressions on their faces, they mean to give us grief." Addy set the enamel coffee pot on the stove.

Grandpa leaned back in his chair, his eyes closed and mouth moving.

She bet he was praying.

She watched as Jess addressed the men when they stepped out of the squad car. "Come on in and spell yourselves for a while. Got some coffee brewing. George is up and ready to meet you."

Hamilton cleared his voice. "Can't stay long. Our business is quite brief."

She rearranged the curtain on the window, then faced the door and waited for it to open. Jess walked in first, then Hamilton, and last, the sheriff.

Grandpa's hospitality kicked in. "Good to see you, Hamilton. It's a bright day outside. Did you see the fields all cleared of this year's beet crop?"

"Heard that a crew of hobos and troublemakers invaded your spread yesterday. Does seem that they accomplished a lot. The sheriff is here to make sure the transfer of your payment is done in a civil manner."

"Wouldn't do it any other way." Grandpa reached into his side pocket and pulled out a roll of bills. "Got the contract with you? I want this to be done to the letter of the law."

"Right here. Need two thousand dollars today, Mr. Meyers. Not a penny less." Hamilton clipped his words.

"Well, I got that and not a penny more for you." Grandpa laid out the bills in fifties and hundreds.

Jess watched the sheriff. The law man stood military straight, a holstered gun at his side.

"Need someone to sign that the rancher handed over the correct amount of money. Sheriff?"

Hamilton held out a pen. "Count the cash, then sign on the middle line."

The strident sound of the sheriff's boot heels on wooden flooring worried Addy. She fussed with the seam on her dress as the sheriff flipped through the bills, then wrote his name on the form.

Hamilton pulled a wallet out of his suit's inner pocket. Carefully, he slid the money in the folds of the leather tooling. Then he folded the contract. He placed both back into his pin-striped suit's pocket.

"What about Miss Meyers's salary?" Jess stood.

"What about it?"

"When will the script be turned into legal tender?" Jess glanced at Hamilton, then fixed his gaze on the sheriff. "Are there laws regulating that?"

The sheriff puckered his lips. "The school board has thirty days to get the cash for the teachers who are being paid in script. They will be able to use a lien on the next year's taxes."

Hamilton hooded his eyes. "Are we through here?"

"Thanks for coming out since I'm not feelin' good. 'Spect that I'll be up-to-date in m' payments from now on." Grandpa raised his mug in salute.

Addy exhaled when they left. She hadn't realized that she had been holding her breath.

Before long, the men and women from Hooverville drove into the yard. She stood on the porch and watched as they set up a metal tripod over a rocked-in fire pit. Soon, an iron pot with water hung from it. She put in four chopped carrots and two quartered potatoes. Others added onions, a hand full of herbs, summer squash, green beans, barley, kernels of corn, diced tumbleweed leaves. A bowl of dried bread cut into croutons and a dish of goat's cheese sat on a small table to garnish the soup.

Murphy and his kin arrived just as the pot started to heat up. True to his word, he brought mutton bones and freshly chopped meat. He slipped it into the pot, letting Calvin stir with a large metal spoon. Mrs. Murphy carried a pottery bowl full of tumbleweed salad. A muslin cloth covered the top.

Addy opened the door. "Just place the salad over here." She directed her to the side table which already held a Ritz cracker apple pie and a plate of molasses cookies. "I look forward to sampling some tumbleweeds. Your husband bragged about how tasty they are."

The hard lines in Mrs. Murphy's leathered face softened. "It's the vinegar dressing that makes it so good."

"Bring in the quilting form." Grace shouted out the door to the Hooverville men.

Two men carried a wooden frame meant for a single size quilt, or nine squares, into the living room. The women gathered around it.

Grace took charge. "Do you have the backing material?"

"I have some sugar sacks that we can use." Addy brought out her fabric. "We'll have to piece it together to fit on the frame, I guess."

"No problem. Viola and Ina will hand stitch them together while we cut the posts and styles. I see you have the material for that from some feed bags they got at the grain store. I have the same pattern of yellow sunflowers."

Reaching into pockets of their flour sack aprons, the five women surrounding Addy pulled out scissors and small tape measures. Before long, all the pieces needed to finish the quilt were cut and sewn onto the squares. The women stretched the bottom of the quilt on the frame, covered it with the cotton batting, then added the top.

I have no idea how to finish this quilt. Please don't ask me to do any more with it. "I'll make biscuits to eat with the mutton stew."

"We can tie this quilt up in no time, if you don't mind." Grace spoke as she threaded a needle.

"No, I don't care. I really would rather bake than sew any day."

Viola gave Addy a warm hug. "Then get baking, and we'll get tying. Hmm. These Sunbonnet Sues and Overall Sams are well stitched. I knew your grandmother, Addy. She'd be real proud of you."

Grandma. Proud of her. Try as she might, Addy failed to keep the tears from leaking out of the corners of her eyes.

Mrs. Murphy joined her at the baking station. "I like to bake when there's enough flour. Let me help you."

"We sure will have to make a lot of biscuits." Addy handed a mixing bowl to Mrs. Murphy.

"I can make Irish soda bread if you want. It's been a while, but it would make a treat for the men. We haven't tasted it for a long time." Mrs. Murphy worried the hem of her apron. "That is, if you can spare the ingredients."

"Those men worked hard yesterday. They saved this homestead. We will celebrate that fact today with Irish soda bread. What do you need?"

"Do you have buttermilk?"

Addy shook her head.

"No matter. If I put some vinegar in milk, it'll be buttermilk by the time the other ingredients are ready." Mrs. Murphy poured vinegar in a cup of milk. "Now, where's the flour?"

Addy watched as the woman measured the dry ingredients, being careful not to waste even a puff of flour. She spread bacon grease into Grandma's metal pans with her fingers.

Mrs. Murphy grasped the mixing bowl and demonstrated how to stir the wet and dry ingredients together. She laid the dough in the bread pans.

"Now, I take a knife and carve the sign of the cross on the top. It's a tradition that has been passed from generation to generation in the Irish kitchens. The bread tastes better if you do this."

Addy made the next batch of Irish soda bread while Mrs. Murphy guided her through the process. The constant chatter of the women who circled the quilting frame provided a background of complaints and advice. Using the strings that tied the burlap bags, the women tied up the quilt at the corners of the Sunbonnet Sue squares. Then, they stitched the binding to the top of the quilt.

Many hands make light work. Wasn't that what Grandma always said?

Addy wore her grandmother's feed-sack apron like a mantle passing a legacy of trusting God from one generation to the next.

The morning and afternoon blended into one long day of eating stew sopped up with Irish soda bread and biscuits. Mrs. Murphy's tumbleweed salad provided a treat for the taste buds as well as nourishment for the body. Several jello molds quickly disappeared. Oatmeal cookies with raisins rounded out the food fest around the tripod fire pit. The men brought buckets and boards to sit upon. RiverLyn, Billy, and Merle played baseball tag, then settled into another game of Monopoly.

Jess sidled over to Addy. "May I have some coffee?"

She poured it into a mug and handed it to him. "Will I see you later this evening?"

"Count on it." He blew across the rim of the mug and winked.

"Addy." Grace called from the quilting frame. "We need your help."

Addy and Mrs. Murphy gathered at the quilting bee for the final stitching while several women from Hooverville took over perking coffee and serving the men. The stitchers' fingers flew in tiny, repetitive motions along the pinned binding. She marveled at the easy way the women pulled thread through fabric without leaving a trace. She copied their movements, and soon developed her own rhythm. By the time that the men ambled in from outside to collect their women and dishes, the finished product was on display.

"Tell the men folk what each of these squares represent, Addy. Talk about your quilt."

With hats in hand, the Hooverville men stood with the rough-handed kin of Patrick Murphy. Jess leaned on the wall among them. All attention focused on her, now holding the quilt.

"Well, this square is for my Grandma, whose fabric stash I am using. This one is Grandpa's square and has bits of his clothing in it. RiverLyn and Billy each have a square that uses the clothing they wore when they were adopted by my grandparents." Addy pointed. "This Overall Sam has material that was given to me when I visited Hooverville. I never want to forget the people there. This Sunbonnet Sue represents all the children who have suffered from dust pneumonia."

Her voice turned raspy. She cleared her throat. "Calvin, do you recognize yourself and the guitar you play at the services on Sunday? This last square is for Jess, who has helped our family in so many ways. Scraps and pieces all stitched together by the women of this community. I will cherish the legacy that this quilt represents." She fought the moisture in her eyes.

A hush fell across the room as her words united the group in a new way.

Grandpa George stood. "Now, did everyone get paid? I can't say how grateful I am for all the laborin' each of ya did to help me git outta trouble."

"You gave us a chance to work. All we wanted was a job." Calvin put his arm around his wife as she smoothed the skirt of her flour-sack dress. "With the money we earned, most of the residents of Hooverville will be able to move to California to start a new life. We appreciate the opportunity you gave us."

Nods from the crowd joined praises to God.

Murphy slapped his knee and guffawed. "My boys and me jest wanted to make sure that the little man won over the bank. You know. Like from the Good Book. David and Goliath."

"Well, we couldn't have done it without all of you." Jess indicated the men and women standing shoulder to shoulder in the room.

"We got one song to sing to y'all before we leave. It's a tune by a man named Woody Guthrie. Goes like this. 'So long, it's been good to know ya. So long, it's been good to know ya.'" Calvin started to wave as he slid out the door with his wife, the words to the song following him as the Hooverville crowd made their way to their vehicles.

"My folks don't sing, but we'll give an Irish blessing." Murphy held up his gnarled, rough hand.

"May the road rise up to meet you,
May the wind be always at your back,
May the sun shine warm on your face,
And the rains fall soft upon your fields,
And until we meet again
May God hold you in the hollow of His hand."

Addy watched from the window as the sheep ranchers' boots kicked up dust clouds across the yard and the Murphy clan headed for the horses and buggies in the barn yard. Grandpa George, Billy, and RiverLyn sat on the porch steps and ate molasses cookies, chuckling over the events of the day.

Addy glowed from the friendship she experienced and a faith deepened by the actions of so many. Proof that God cared and could be trusted with life's problems. Just like Grandpa and Grandma always proclaimed.

Across the room, Jess put his coffee mug on the table, then sauntered to her. Her heart beat harder than Mrs. Murphy mixing Irish soda bread. Jess raised her chin with his blistered fingers. His kiss lasted so long that her knees almost buckled. She melted into Jess's muscular arms, listening to the rapid beat of his heart.

"Addy Meyers, will you do me the honor of being my wife?" Jess whispered in her ear. The warmth of his breath tickled her neck.

"I was hoping that you would ask." She held him close. "Yes, I will."

A barn owl hooted in the cottonwood tree. The night wind cooled the air. Kerosene lamps spread shadowy light throughout the room. Wrapped in the coziness of the Sunbonnet Sue and Overall Sam quilt, Addy and Jess spoke of new memories they would be making.

Together.

Questions for Book Clubs

- Describe Addy. What are her dreams and goals? What impedes her progress toward her heart's desires?
- Describe Grandpa's situation and compare it to the homesteaders near him.
- Discuss the classroom dynamics that challenge Addy. How did playing baseball lead to a resolution? Would that technique work today?
- As the book progresses, many of the dishes that the folk ate in the 1930's are presented. Are these Grandma's recipes, or are still they served on contemporary tables?
- How did River Lyn and Billy join Grandpa's family?
- What is the orphan train? How is Jess connected to the orphan train?
- Try to paint a word picture of Hooverville and its residents.
- Explain the significance of community canning kitchens in the Dust Bowl.
- Why does everyone want justice?

- The metaphor of scraps, left-overs, fragments and remnants relates to life in the Dust Bowl. How does it play out in our own everyday life?

If you need more resources, find my website and blog at:
www.cleolampos.com

The Quilts of the 1930 Dust Bowl Era

Chapter 1- **Sunbonnet Sue**- Taken from a series of books published in early 1900's, the illustrator, Bertha Corbett Melcher is credited with the iconic Sunbonnet quilting designs. The stitched images of Sunbonnet Sue and Overall Sam represented brighter and sunnier days during the hard years of the Depression.

Chapter 2-**Butterflies**- The 1930 Oklahoma song "I'll Fly Away" mirrors a desire to be free from problems. Quilters picked up this image by stitching butterflies, which became an easy way to use up scrap materials and incorporate a bit of embroidery. The yearning to escape the difficulties of the day may have made these free fluttering butterflies so popular.

Chapter 3-**Sunbonnet Sue**-With her chunky design, Sunbonnet Sue adapted to every season, and many occupations, including teacher in a one room schoolhouse. Appliqued extras give the square a bit more detail.

Chapter 4-**Log Cabin**- A popular design dating back to the Civil War and symbolizing home. The color of the center square is significant. Red center symbolized the hearth of the home while a yellow center represented a welcoming light in the window. A Log Cabin quilt with a black center hanging on a clothesline invited runaway slaves to stop in the safe house on the Underground Railroad.

Chapter 5-**Sunbonnet Sue**- Sunbonnet Sue's bulky shape lends to the addition of embroidered details to change the basic design into a unique quilt square. Buttons, rickrack, lace, and other objects were sewn on as embellishments that reflected the stitcher's individuality.

Chapter 6-**Schoolhouse Quilt**-According to the International Quilt Study Center in Nebraska, "for rural women, teaching was both the most prestigious and the highest paying opportunity available to them." A home that values education and the teachers who taught in the rural one-room schoolrooms. Maybe that is what this pattern represented to many women as they hand stitched the schoolhouse cut-outs into blocks, and tied the top to the backing.

Chapter 7-**Overall Sam**- Like his counterpart, Sunbonnet Sue, Overall Sam was a popular character in the reading series *Sunbonnet Babies* and *the Overall Boys* which took place in Holland, Italy and Switzerland. Overall Sam is joined by Farmer Bill, Fisherman Fred, and Dutch Boy. All these variations exist in quilts from the 1930's, including a cowboy version.

Chapter 8-**Dresden Plate**-One of the most widely quilted pattern of the Great Depression. The fabric is easy to date because the Dresden Plate utilized the floral prints of the period gleaned from feed sacks. The name for this design reflects the romance of the Victorian Era and the beautiful plates from Dresden, Germany's porcelain industry. A longing for beauty and connection to a time of elegance during a decade of despair may account for this pattern's universal appeal.

Chapter 9-**Overall Sam**- This versatile basic cut used up fabrics from the denim, corduroy, or tweeds that created men's wear. Add a little applique or embroidery and the square had an appealing look.

Chapter 10-**Grandparent versions**-Age did not deter the Sunbonnet Sue and Overall Sam patterns from being used. Babies, children, adults, and, yes, grandparents all fit the mold.

Chapter 11-**Fan Quilt** -Dress fabrics being sold in the 1930's were pastel colors-pinks, blues, yellows, oranges, and very fine, small prints. It was a way to take people away from the gloom of their situation. After creating clothes from the lively materials, the scraps were repurposed into quilts. The newspapers printed patterns, like the Fan, to use up all the left over pieces. The color range of a quilt makes it easy to tell if it was made in the Depression Era.

Chapter 12-**Sunbonnet Sue-** Every little girl enjoyed watching her mother take the extra pieces of a new sugar sack dress to create another square on the Sunbonnet Sue quilt. As the top of the quilt grew, the memories of the clothes the child wore were stitched into the fabric of the family's life. Functional and sentimental, these quilts traveled over the years for many women.

Chapter 13-**String Quilts**-The WPA(Works Projects Administration) collected narratives in the 1930s and discovered that after the Civil War, African American women went to work as domestics. Scraps from sewing, discarded clothing and feed sacks were given to these women who cut the materials into long strips and sewed them together with a solid color running diagonally on the square. The strong design of the String Quilts produced stunning results.

Chapter 14-**Sheep Applique**-Repeated patterns of animals in different fabrics and colors resulted in creative quilts. Scotty dogs were popular, as were other farm yard animals like chickens and sheep. The swatches traded at the Snack and Swap get-togethers helped to give variety and texture to the appliqued flock that the Colorado sheepherders tended in the foothills of the Rocky Mountains.

Chapter 15-**Hobo Overall Sam**-So many quilts were stitched from the rough and tumble textures of chicken feed bags or flour sacks. The hobos who roamed two million strong across the United States seeking employment reflected that look. But quilts are about coming together and having a quilting bee that fixes the layers of fabric together. The kind of community that hobos longed for as they rode the rails in search of home.

Chapter 16-**Overall Sam**-The Bible in the hand of this Overall Sam represents the dependence on faith by those who suffered loss of everything in the decade of the '30's. The songs, "Precious Lord, Take My Hand", and "Will the Circle

Be Unbroken?" mirror the depth of the feelings of people as Black Blizzards turned grassland into hard pan in the Oklahoma Panhandle.

Chapter 17-**Nine Patch**-The Nine Patch is a very simple block, just nine squares of cloth that make a square. But it is also a "block type" that describes the style of the construction. Using a Nine Patch style, the quilter can easily create a Roman Square, Churn Dash, Shoo Fly, Jacob's Ladder, Maple Leaf and Winged Square quilt. Teaching a child to sew this pattern unleashed a world of creativity through variation.

Chapter 18-**Musical Overall Sam**- The addition of a guitar to the staple pattern brings the legendary Woody Guthrie to life. As he wandered the United States, he wrote "This Land is Your Land". Sitting in a dust storm so dense he couldn't see his hand in front of his eyes, Woody wrote, "So Long". Spokesman for the migrant workers who wanted fair treatment, Woody Guthrie symbolizes the struggles of the Dust Bowl times.

Chapter 19-**Sunbonnet Sue**- Kitchen tools in hand, Sunbonnet Sue can rustle up a plate of tumble weed leaves for her family. Depression cooking meant a lot of oatmeal, casseroles, biscuits and gravy, beans, and Jell-O. Just like quilting used up scraps of fabric, so did the culinary creations utilize scraps of food at frugal meals. "Use it up, wear it out. Make it do or do without."

Last quilt square-**Double Wedding Ring Quilt**-This quilt used a good deal of solid fabric that had to be purchased for the background of the wedding ring, an expense that many Depression Era families could not afford. Therefore, the Double Wedding Ring was usually made up for display or special occasion use. Children were not allowed to jump or play on this one. A difficult quilt to make, it is not the design for a novice. An heirloom for sure.

Introducing the Author

Although born in 1946, Cleo Lampos' life mirrors so many aspects of the 1930's culture. Born in Greeley, Colorado, she experienced a few minor dust storms as a child. Her father, Jess, owned a dragline business that dug irrigation ditches for beet farmers and spud cellars for ranchers. The stories of the Dust Bowl were handed down to Lampos through her mother and several boxes of letters that span the years of 1930-1942. Lampos has spent many years researching the topics related to the Dust Bowl era. She realized that her childhood was based on "use it up, wear it out, make it do, or do without."

Quilting preoccupied not only Lampos' mother, but all the aunts, extended family, friends and church groups. Embroidery projects came in second. Over the years, Lampos has created several quilts, taken classes, and joined the Stitchers Group in Oak Lawn, Illinois. The women in the group helped Lampos and her sixteen-year-old granddaughter to finish a state bird and flower quilt started by Lampos' mother from feedbag muslin and sugar sack material. Currently, Kaeley Clark sleeps under the quilt of love started by her great-grandmother, embroidered by her grandmother, and stitched by herself.

Joyce Beenes created a Sunbonnet Sue and Overall Sam quilt for Lampos to use when she speaks to college extension classes, senior centers, or sewing guilds about fabrics of the 1930's. Lampos and her husband can, dehydrate and freeze vegetables from their urban farmette in an attempt to be frugal and eat organic food with a low food milage. They volunteer in two community gardens in the pantry section where the produce is donated to the city's food pantries.

OTHER BOOKS BY CLEO LAMPOS

A Mother's Song Historical novel about orphan trains and Irish immigration

Teachers of Diamond Project School Series
Miss Bee and the Do Bee- Special education teacher faces challenges
Second Chances- First year teacher in urban setting
Cultivating Wildflowers-Gifted teacher learns valuable less**ons**

Rescuing Children-Accounts of persons in 1800's-1900 who rescued waifs
Grandpa's Remembering Book-Family friendly book about Alzheimer's

Teaching Diamonds in the Tough- Memoirs of Lampos' teaching career

Enjoy reading these books and write a review on amazon.com

Made in the USA
Lexington, KY
27 December 2018